Sarah Lucy McKay

Lucy, the Sold Orphan

A Drama from Real Life

Sarah Lucy McKay

Lucy, the Sold Orphan
A Drama from Real Life

ISBN/EAN: 9783337343194

Printed in Europe, USA, Canada, Australia, Japan

Cover: Foto ©Andreas Hilbeck / pixelio.de

More available books at **www.hansebooks.com**

LUCY

THE ✦ SOLD ✦ ORPHAN

A DRAMA FROM REAL LIFE.
IN 12 ACTS.

BY ✦ MRS. ✦ SARAH ✦ LUCY ✦ McKAY

BAY CITY, MICH.
1882.

DESCRIPTIONS.

DESCRIPTION OF ACT I.

MRS. LILLABRIDGE in her parlor.

MRS. LILLABRIDGE, when first seen, is dressed in the style of 1858. Her dress is made of seal-brown material, the skirt being plain, but full. The waist is also plain, having long flowing sleeves, trimmed with black point lace. Her collar is trimmed with embroidery, the front and back having deep points. Her hair is brought down over her ears, then done up in a chignon in the back. Her appearance is to be graceful.

LUCY'S DESCRIPTION.

LUCY'S appearance is like a school girl aged 14 years, with her books in her arm.

Her dress is made of Scotch plaid, the skirt being straight and full. The trimming is three rows of ribbon-velvet of a contrasting shade. The waist is plain, with large flowing sleeves. Her hat is a flat leghorn shape, with long ties in the back. Her hair is in curls, beginning at the forehead. Her appearance must be easy and graceful.

DESCRIPTION OF DR. PFEIFER.

DR. PFEIFER is of medium height, having a large red face, and a peaked nose. His eyes are blue and very large, having an ugly expression. His hair is light, the back being cut straight across his neck. His head is uncommon large; the top is entirely bald. He wears a red mustache and a spear of chin-whiskers. His spectacles are gold-banded. His hat is a large buckwheat slouch, and faded. His boots are large and awkward, and his vest is made of light-green velvet, wearing with it a long dress-coat of a darker shade, and narrow through the shoulders. The pants are striped, brown and black. His left shoulder he carries higher than the right one, and his walk is very quick, exhibiting his ill-temper. His gold-headed cane he strikes down when talking with any one, so as to be understood. He tries to be polite with all he says, but spoils it by acting awkward, and misunderstanding each person. Whenever entering MRS. LILLA-BRIDGE'S parlor, or departing, he makes an awkward display with his cane. Whenever passing before MRS. LILLABRIDGE or LUCY, without excusing himself, he steps on their feet in an awkward manner.

DESCRIPTION OF SCENE II., ACT I.

LUCY in her bed-room.

MRS. LILLABRIDGE and LUCY are dressed the same as in Scene I.

DESCRIPTION OF SCENE III., ACT I.

MRS. LILLABRIDGE is again knitting in her parlor.

Her dress is made of changeable blue silk. The skirt is full, having two rows of black lace around it. The waist is tight-fitting, and is trimmed with one row of black lace extending over the shoulders. The sash is made up of the same silk that the dress is, and trimmed around the edges with black lace. In the back it is tied in a straight, careless loop. Her sleeves are long and flowing, the edges being trimmed with narrow lace.

DESCRIPTION OF LUCY.

LUCY appears in a dove-colored silk dress. The skirt is ruffled from the bottom up to the waist. Her waist is made like an old-style Quaker waist, having short sleeves with one ruffle on the bottom of each. The neck is cut low. Under the dress-sleeves are worn embroidered muslin sleeves. The neck has muslin ruching set in very deep. On her hair and bosom a white rose is worn. The slippers match the dress. Over her lace mitts plain gold wristlets are worn.

DESCRIPTION OF DR. PFEIFER.

The DOCTOR is dressed in a black suit—the coat being long and too large through the shoulders. He carries the cane as before, and acts awkward in his manner. He wears a turned-down collar and a black neck-tie. On his head a plug hat is worn.

The COLORED SERVANT GIRL is dressed in plain black, wearing a white apron.

DESCRIPTION OF MR. LILLABRIDGE.

MR. LILLABRIDGE has a graceful appearance, and wears black clothes.

THE MINISTER.

The MINISTER is dressed in black and wears a white neck-tie.

DESCRIPTION OF ACT II.

MRS. LUCY PFEIFER'S kitchen is furnished with a cook-stove, three wooden bottom chairs and one wooden rocking chair. The table is arranged for tea, having a white linen spread, fine porcelain ware, silver cake-baskets, napkin rings and all belonging to a set. The cradle is near the table, with the little infant in it. The kitchen is curtained off enough so as to see the bed-room. This all must show the contrast between her own home and the one that the Doctor provides her.

DESCRIPTION OF LUCY.

LUCY'S dress is made plain and of brown dotted calico. With this is worn a long white apron and a pointed collar.

DESCRIPTION OF DR. PFEIFER.

DR. PFEIFER looks the same as when he was married. He wears the same black clothes and a hair watch-chain mounted with gold. When sitting at the table he rests the cane on his knees.

DESCRIPTION OF THE DUTCH BAKER.

The DUTCH BAKER is fleshy, wearing a stubby beard and side-whiskers. On his head is worn a paper cap made of flour-sacking, allowing some letters to be seen. His pants are linen, and his vest and coat black woolen. His coat, vest and wooden-soled slippers are sprinkled with flour.

THE BAKER'S WIFE.

The BAKER'S WIFE is a fleshy and jolly-looking Dutch woman. Her cheeks are full and rosy, and her hair is combed plain and done up in Dutch braids. Her dress is made of dark brown, coarse goods; the skirt being very short, and the waist loose, without any sleeves, except white ones, reaching nearly to the elbow. Around her neck is worn a large white handkerchief, with the ends tucked under the belt of her black apron. A cardinal silk handkerchief is folded and extended around her forehead, then tied at the back of her neck. On her feet brogan shoes are worn.

DESCRIPTION OF ACT III.

The coal-pits may be arranged so that it is dim by having jack lanterns hung on the branches of trees. The smoke must be boiling from the vent-holes. The surroundings are snow-banks, rocks, and dried oak trees. On the snow dried leaves and coal are scattered in every direction.

JIM must be busy with raking the coal together and singing Irish ballads.

To imitate thunder the storm may be played on the piano—the part only that sounds like thunder. The howling winds and the rustling of leaves may be imitated by forcing air through cylinders.

DESCRIPTION OF IRISH JIM.

IRISH JIM has on a blue frock, brown overalls and a black cap, and is busy working with his rake. When MRS. PFEIFER enters, JIM must peer between the banks as if to say, " Who is that?"

DESCRIPTION OF MRS. PFEIFER.

MRS. PFEIFER has on the same dress that she wore when seen in her kitchen. The infant is tied to her back with a shawl over it, and MRS. PFEIFER has one around herself. In her right hand she has her Bible, and in the left an extra shawl. The bottom of her dress is wet, as if she had been making her way through wet snow.

DESCRIPTION OF ACT IV.

The DOCTOR's office has in it a book-case, a writing-desk and a medicine-rack on which are small labeled bottles. The DOCTOR has his spectacles on, and a brown suit of clothes with a white vest. The word " profession" he uses with such an emphasis as if he thinks it is edifying.

PATIENTS.

FELIX appears like a ruffian, MIKE like a chore-boy, and CRAWFORD like a polished young man. The PEASANT is very rough-looking. The MAN with the bandaged arm looks prim.

MRS. PFEIFER.

MRS. PFEIFER, with her infant, enters the office looking the same as she did when among the coal-pits.

DESCRIPTION OF JIM.

JIM is dressed the same when he enters the office as he was when tending the coal-pits.

DESCRIPTION OF ACT V.

The milliner shop is arranged with a show-case and a long table with revolving-racks for the bonnets.

When the girls enter they must busy themselves by trimming hats. MRS. PFEIFER must trim as if she is in a hurry when the DOCTOR enters.

The shop-girls wear black dresses and white aprons.

MRS. PFEIFER wears a heavy trimmed silk dress, with a gold watch-chain and a set of high-priced jewelry. Her appearance must be as if she possessed great business faculties.

For the infant a large wax doll may be had, with a bonnet on its head, so that the difference could not easily be distinguished.

DESCRIPTION OF THE DOCTOR.

The DOCTOR, when entering the milliner shop, must be strutting, with his cane under one arm and a cucumber in each hand. He is to wear a plug hat, and a black coat and vest with light-checked pants that are too large for him. His feet must be as awkward as before. For the cucumbers wooden ones may be used.

AUNTIE FLAGAN.

AUNTIE FLAGAN is to wear a light-green dress, the skirt being made too short, and the waist without a seam in the back and only one dart on each side. Around her neck a yellow handkerchief is to be worn, having the ends in front tucked under the belt of her straight yellow apron. Her hair is done up in a hair net, and a narrow band of light-green ribbon is tied at one side and formed in a loop. She is to be broad-shouldered and very robust.

DESCRIPTION OF SCENE II., ACT V.

The angels that MRS. PFIEFER had seen when in her trance-like dream were robed in white, and had glistening, outstretched wings and golden hair. These could be attached to some stiff wire, and the stage could be darkened so as to have the clouds represented like real ones. The hawk and the dove may be stuffed and fixed in a way that they would turn their heads.

This was a reality. The dove flew in one time when MRS. PFEIFER was sick, and AUNTIE FLAGAN, her nurse, was present. The hawk was a pet of little JOHNNY PFEIFER'S, and flew in the time when the DOCTOR bled her arm, after frightening her so as to cause her fainting. These two occurrences should be joined together in one scene, so as to beautify it.

ACT VI.

The dinner-table for New Year's day is to be arranged with silver ware, having a turkey in the center, and some cream cake, made in layers like jelly cake.

DR. PFEIFER.

DR. PFEIFER is to be dressed very neat on New Year's day, wearing his spectacles and letting his cane rest on his knees when sitting at the table.

MISS MAMIE is to wear a dinner dress and FAIRY is to wear a blue princess suit.

MAMIE is a young lady, and FAIRY is about nine or ten years of age. Little JOHNNY must have light hair and in ringlets. He is to wear a sailor suit.

MRS. PFEIFER is to wear a dinner dress, and have her hair in waves in the front and done up in a coil in the back.

DESCRIPTION OF ACT VII.

The bar-room is to be arranged in the German style, having the beer-kegs and the wine-bottles show.

THE DUTCH BAR-KEEPER.

The bar-keeper is a large, fleshy man, wearing no coat, and his shirt sleeves are rolled up. On his head is worn a red flannel cap, its shape being similar to a dunce-cap, and on the end is a red tassel. On his feet he wears wooden-soled slippers, having only a strip of leather over the toes.

THE DOCTOR.

THE DOCTOR is dressed in the bar-room scene in checked pants and a long linen coat. He wears a plug hat and his spectacles. His cane he carries under his arm. When first entering the bar-room he has each of his children by the hand.

FAIRY lingers by herself to read a book.

JOHNNY is to be dressed in a light suit, wearing with it a sailor hat.

FAIRY is to be dressed in a blue muslin dress, wearing with it a light gray sack with side pockets.

ACT VIII.—DESCRIPTIONS.

THE PIC-NIC.

The trees are close together where there are no pic-nic tables. Beyond the tables are lemonade and beer stands.

The DOCTOR and his children have one table. At the other table young Dutch girls and young men are drinking and eating bolognas and fried cakes. The DOCTOR and children are dressed the same as they were in the bar-room before they started for the pic-nic.

HANS, the waiter, is to wear a long, white apron, and appear jolly.

ACT IX.—DESCRIPTIONS.

MRS. PFEIFER is washing in her wash-room, having her infant in one arm, and washing with one hand. Her dress looks shabby.

JOHNNY and FAIRY enter returning from the pic-nic, and the DOC-
TOR's plug hat looks the same as it did when he left the pic-nic.

DESCRIPTION OF SCENE II.

MRS. PFEIFER, with her infant in her arm, is crossing a stream of
water. The planks are only ten or twelve inches wide, and tip from
one side to the other when MRS. PFEIFER is crossing, showing that
she is escaping danger. She suddenly peers between the distant
rocks, when almost on the other side, then she shouts in a frightened
tone, "Oh, children, come quick! before our pa comes after us!"
Then JOHNNY grasps his mother's hand, and FAIRY grasps at her
mother's dress. When reaching the other side of the stream, their
clothes are to be dripping wet.

AUNTIE FLAGAN IN ACT IX.

AUNTIE FLAGAN'S countenance is the same as when seen in the
milliner shop. Her dress this time is a dark brown calico, made like
a kitchen dress. Over this is worn a long yellow apron. Around her
neck is a white handkerchief tied loosely. On her head a light green
cloth scarf is worn. Her shoes are heavy brogans.

ACT X.

The DOCTOR is still lying on the kitchen floor, where he fell at
MRS. PFEIFER's feet. His hat is on the floor and jammed. When
arousing from his drunken stupor, he is to act as if to say, " Where
am I?"

ACT XI.

MRS. PFEIFER with her two daughters in her parlor. The cush-
ioned furniture is covered with deep cardinal plush.

MISS MAMIE, the young lady who is at the piano, is to be dressed
in a fashionable house dress, and MRS. PFEIFER also.

FAIRY is to be dressed in a pink princess dress, wearing with it a
pale blue sash.

Little JOHNNY, when entering the parlor, is to have his school-
books under his arm. He is to wear a sailor suit and hat.

DOCTOR PFEIFER is to wear his spectacles, a long gray duster
and a straw hat. His cane is to be carried in his hand during the
whole act. His boots are to be long and narrow.

COUNT MARTRIT is to have curly hair, and his clothes are to be
fashionable.

ACT XII.—SCENE I.

MRS. PFEIFER is to be resting on a couch, having her three children by her side. The children are to be dressed differently from what
they were when in the parlor. MRS. PFEIFER is to wear a loose-fitting
house dress.

LAWYER HOGAL is to have the appearance of a business man.

SCENE II.

The lawyer's office is to be arranged so that people will know it is
his office.

MRS. PFEIFER and daughters, when entering, are to be dressed in
street costumes.

The assistant lawyer is to appear, when entering with the papers,
as if he had been writing.

LUCY,

THE SOLD ORPHAN.

— —

ACT I.

CHARACTERS—1. MRS. LILLABRIDGE. 3. DR. PFEIFER.
2. MISS LUCY RHODES. 4. REV. MR. BALL.
5. THE COLORED SERVANT GIRL.

SCENE I.

MRS. LILLABRIDGE is seen in a sitting-room near a table, knitting.

Enter LUCY.

MRS. LILLABRIDGE. [To LUCY.] Have you seen Dr. Pfeifer to-day, Lucy?

LUCY. Oh! no, Auntie. Please do not talk to me about that horrible man. [SITTING DOWN.] He is such a rough, old and ugly looking German, I can't bear to look at him.

MRS. LILLABRIDGE. Oh, hush! hush, Lucy! [VERY CALM.] You do not know who you are referring to. I beg—you do not consider. He is such a rich and learned physician; and then, you know, it is so grand to marry into some rich foreign family, where you shall have wealth, honor and station in life. And you—little blue-eyed darling—with such a good and Christian spirit, will soon subdue all that seems rough within that German's heart.

LUCY. [OUT OF PATIENCE.] Oh, dear Auntie! although I am gentle, meek and loving, and try to be a Christian, Christians you know, Auntie, never could tame lions, and that man is truly a lion.

DR. PFEIFER enters. [LUCY acts frightened.]

DR. P. Coot tay, latties; coot tay, latties. [RUBBING HIS HANDS.] Vat iss der matter mit your toor pell? I shake avay, und shake avay, und it makes notting for a noise. Make dot somedings oud, I valks ride in. I hafe pen looking after my profession. [MRS. LILLABRIDGE arises very unconcerned.

MRS. LILL. [To THE DR.] Certainly not, Doctor; walk in. [THE DOCTOR APPROACHES MISS LUCY. MRS. LILL. INTRODUCES LUCY.] Dr. Pfeifer, my neice, Miss Lucy Rhodes.

Lucy. [Bowing.] How do you do, Dr. Pfeifer?

Dr. [Looking at the Aunt.] Vat iss it? Vat, vat did you say der name vass?

Aunt. Lucy Rhodes is the name.

The Doctor. [To Lucy, very pleased.] Oh, Lucy! Lucy, dot pe a pooty name. Shust tinck vance off dot vash Lucy Pfeifer. Vouldn't I feel so heppy? Hay!   [The Aunt acts pleased. Lucy
                                                    tries to withdraw from the room.

Aunt. [Calling Lucy back.] Can't you stay and entertain Dr. Pfeifer?

Lucy. [Coming back.] How can I entertain him? He can't even speak the American language.

Aunt. Be still! Can't you show him your books and music?

Lucy. Certainly, Auntie, if it be your wish, I shall with pleasure. [Lucy hurriedly shows Doctor books from the table, and sits down.

The Doctor. [Not looking at the books, keeps them in his hands, merely saying:] Dose are pooty books.

                                        [Lucy starts as if going to another room.

The Aunt. [To Lucy.] Be still! Can't you sit down, Lucy? The Doctor will tell you all about Europe.

Lucy. [Angrily.] He can't. The old Dutchman don't talk so that a living soul can understand what he is saying.

Aunt. [Very pleasing.] But, my own little dear, do as I bid you. You shall be rewarded by getting that beautiful blue silk dress.

Lucy. Oh, please, my dear Aunt, do not talk about him to me. He is so hideous. I don't care for silk dresses. I only wish to be good.

Aunt. [To Lucy.] I am sure you would not be good if you disobey your dead mamma's desire to have you obey Auntie in all things.

Lucy. Oh, Auntie, did mamma mean for me to marry a man I dislike to please you?

Aunt. Oh, do be quiet. Be excused from my presence and go to your room.

Lucy. [To the Doctor.] Excuse me, sir.   [Departs.

Aunt. [Calling Lucy.] Wait a moment. I wish to tell you I shall talk with Dr. Pfeifer. [Indignantly.] I have business with him, and no one else. He is to show me credentials proving to me his immense wealth, which I do hope, in, all goodness, some day will be yours, [Lucy acts startled] that you may scatter it broadcast over the land, which seems to be your highest aim, to make others happy.

                                        [The Doctor acts pleased.

Lucy. [Very emphatic.] Indeed, I am sure I never can marry that man—not even to please you. [The Aunt, with her hand over
          Lucy's mouth, leads her from the room. The Doctor
          acts frightened.

                         The Aunt returns.

Doctor. Oh, Mattam Lillapritge! she vass such a pooty gurl, leedle Lucy. [Rising.] She's got sooch pooty shkin and red cheeks, shust like, you know, a leedle tolls. Tot pooty hair, nit sooch a pooty leedle mout, shust like, you know, dose leedle pullfrocks vat 'sing in der leedle bonds in der vinter dimes. [Sorrowful.] Oh, my! it often mate me tream tot I voult like shust like her a vife.

Aunt. [To Doctor.] Sit down, please. [The Doctor sits down and drawing papers from his pocket, reads one of them silently.

Doctor. Oh, Mattam Lillapritge! Look here vonce, Mattam. [Mrs. Lillabridge looks over his shoulder at the papers.] Look! See! [Opening the papers.] Here are dose papers dot make me heir to [pause] two hundert und fifty tousant tollars shust [pause] vone week from to-day; no, yestertay. [Pause.] Yes, tot iss ter tay. [Pointing to the papers.] You see all dose pick plack und red zeals, mit dose pick gounselmen's names shtant on tem dare? [Emphatic.] You see dot iss der vay ve to peeshniss in mine country, hay. You see dot ish der vay der laws are. Und no humbug shtuff, like dose tings fixed up here in America. Shust tinck vonce! Defranchising efery poty vat hafe mit tem to do. It iss awful to tinck vat nations der iss. It seems pooty mooch some dimes dot I ket crasy ven I reat so much apout tem, mit der humbugs vat make notting oud.

Aunt. Very well, Doctor, you shall have the fair Lucy, if all this be true.

Doctor. [Very excited.] True? True? Dot pesh shust so true ash I shtant here mit dose papers, und mit my feet before your heat. Dot pesh shust so true as der Gospel.

Aunt. Very well. Call to-morrow at four, and you shall know your fate.

Doctor. Put off she vont marry me?

Aunt. Consent or not, she must obey me.

Doctor. [Angrily.] Vat? Vat you say? I don't got vone sent? Ven you hafe seen all dose papers in mine hant. Und shust so coot ash so mooch golt. Und for a man off my profession, hay?

Aunt. You did not understand me. I meant she must marry you.

Doctor. [Stammering.] Ox-coo-coose me.

Aunt. Certainly.

Doctor. [Putting on his hat.] Coot tay, Mattam Lillapritge. I gall to-morrow, on der dime you setted me, at four.

[Doctor departs. The Aunt meditates.

Aunt. I wonder what Lucy can be doing I will steal in her room and find out. [Slowly departing.] There is no knowing what children may be doing when they are once crossed in love. [Depart.

SCENE II.—Lucy in a bed-room packing her clothes.

The Aunt enters.

Aunt. Oh, Lucy! what is this for, I pray?

LUCY. [WIPING THE TEARS FROM HER EYES.] Oh, Aunty! I am going to see my poor grandma once more.

AUNT. Oh, no. [DRAWING A LETTER FROM HER POCKET] darling! Here is a letter from grandma stating you shall not come until after she writes again to me.

LUCY. No, indeed, grandma does not mean to, nor want me to stay away. [LOOKING AT THE LETTER.] And besides, this is not grandma's writing.

AUNT. Where do you think I would get the letter, if it's not from grandma?

LUCY. I am sure I can't tell. I am positive that that is not her writing, and I am very much troubled. I cannot stop here. I don't get any more letters from Deloss. I know something must be wrong. He has always been a prompt correspondent until of late. Did you not know that Deloss and I are to be married as soon as I am old enough?

AUNT. [WITH A SNEER.] Oh, law! He is safe off to the war, and you will never hear or see him more.

LUCY. Gone to the war? [SHRINKING BACK.] Oh, cruel Heaven!
[LUCY kneels as if in prayer.

AUNT. Oh! such a stupid child. You never seem to care for money, nor for a man who has it. It is just like you. I am disgusted with your girlish ideas. The Doctor does love you so much, too.

LUCY. Oh! dear me. He is so repulsive and rough in his manner. I am sure he can have no conception of a pure and elevating love.

AUNT. [DEPARTING.] Tut, tut, child! Wait until to-morrow, then you will perhaps see matters in a clearer light.

LUCY. [PRAYING.] Oh, my Father in Heaven, if it be possible, let this bitter cup pass from my lips. But not as my will, but as Thy will in Heaven be done.   [The AUNT departs.

SCENE III.—THE AUNT IS SEWING IN HER SITTING ROOM.

An invisible bell strikes four. LUCY enters.

LUCY. Is it four o'clock yet, Auntie?

AUNT. Yes, the clock struck a moment ago.

DOCTOR enters, rubbing his hands.

DOCTOR. [LOOKING AROUND.] Coot tay, latties. Pooty mooch four o'clock yet, latties?

AUNT. How do you do, Doctor? I am very glad to see you.

DOCTOR. [TO LUCY.] How to, Lucy?

LUCY. Good afternoon, Doctor.

AUNT. [TO DOCTOR.] Have a chair, please. [The DOCTOR, with excitement, places his hat in a chair and sits on it.
LUCY taking the hat places it on the table.

DOCTOR. Oh! latties, I pesh so peesy all der tay, dot I know not off I ket pooty much trew on time or not mit mine profession. You know mine profession keeps me pooty peesy. hay?

AUNT. [To LUCY.] You see, the Doctor has come to see you. Oh, do answer whether you will be his lawful wedded wife or not. Of course, you will say yes. No, you cannot say, and you are to be obedient to all of your friends. Please remember your dead mama's desire. You are to obey those who have you in their care.

LUCY. [TREMBLING.] I must answer, No. *I never can say yes to that man. I never can say yes. I don't like him. I have given my heart to Deloss, and my word I can never take back, though I die in the cause.*   [AUNT departs. LUCY sits down.

DOCTOR. [TRIES TO PUT HIS ARM AROUND LUCY'S NECK. LUCY RESISTS.] Oh, mine leedle Lucy. Shust dell. Dit your Aunt speak somethings apout me of you? Of you vill pe mine fife?

LUCY. [IN A STARTLED TONE.] No, I can never be a wife to you. My heart and hand I have promised to another.

DOCTOR. Coom, shust lofe me vone leedle bit. I lofe you.

LUCY. You? I do not love you, nor ever can.

DOCTOR. [MOTIONING WITH HIS HANDS.] Vat lofe? Dot make nodding oud. Dot ish pooty mooch der same. Dot make no tifference. I lofe you. You lofe not me. I marry you. You marry me, for I peesh rich, und it make no tifference.

LUCY. Oh, no! It would indeed be very wrong to say I love you, for you are so detestable.   [The DOCTOR quickly sits beside a table.

. DOCTOR. Tea table ish ready for me? Vot ish tot? Somedings pooty good to eat? All righd. Pring him on, for I vash so hungry shust now dot I could eat a raw tock. I hafe seen after mine profession.

LUCY. [ASIDE.] Tea table. What does he mean?   [Departs.

AUNT meets LUCY at the door.

AUNT. What is the matter, Lucy?

LUCY. Oh, Auntie! just think, Dr. Pfeifer would like something good to eat. I tell you, that man is insane. I told him he was detestable, when he asked for a tea table and something good to eat.

AUNT. It is a good thing he did not understand you. You know it is the custom in Europe to serve callers with refreshments. Just go back and entertain him while I order a lunch. After you are married and have learned the language, how pleasant your life will be, to be sure.

[AUNT departs. LUCY again seats herself to entertain the DOCTOR.

LUCY. Auntie will be here in a few minutes.

DOCTOR. Dot's all ride. [ENTER AUNT AND SITS NEAR THE DOCTOR. A SERVANT ENTERS WITH SOME WINE AND CAKE.] Oh, mine gracious! Vat, vine, too? [THE DOCTOR TAKING A DOUGHNUT, EXAMINES IT CLOSELY.—To THE AUNT.] My gracious! Mattam Lillapritge, [SHOWING HER THE DOUGHNUT.] vat you call dose leedle round dings, all burnt prown py der sun? Are dey dose preat fruits vat ve reat apout, vat crow on drees?

AUNT. Why, Doctor, they are doughnuts.

DOCTOR. Vat? Chaw-nuts? Tey look coot. [DOCTOR, PUTTING THE DOUGHNUT IN HIS MOUTH, ENDEAVORS TO CRACK IT AS HE WOULD A NUT. IT FLIES OUT IN CRUMBS.] Vel, vel! I nefer see such fine chaw-nuts in mine life, in mine home. Dey crack ride avay so quick. [EATING A PIECE OF CAKE DIPS IT INTO THE WINE; THEN, TURNING HIS HEAD, APPEARS RIDICULOUS AT EACH MOUTHFUL.—TO LUCY, VERY SUDDENLY.] You pe mine fife to-tay, Lucy?

LUCY. No, never! I never could be your wife.

DOCTOR. Vat? You not kife me voue kees?

LUCY. [WITH DISGUST.] No, I have none for you, Doctor. Yet I shall always do right, even if my Aunt compels me to marry you. But from that unhappy day forward, the word love shall never pass my lips. If it did it would be false. You can only have my hand.

DOCTOR. [NODDING HIS HEAD, ACTS PLEASED.] Vel, dot ish ride. Ve vill now be coupled together by law somedimes. I hafe a ride now to claim you ant your keeses.

AUNT. [TO LUCY.] Now, give the Doctor your hand.

LUCY. [GIVING THE DOCTOR HER HAND, SPEAKS WITH INDIGNATION.] Am I a slave that I should be sold to the highest bidder, and my happiness bartered away forever?

AUNT. Why do you talk in that manner, when you are to have a kind husband, and one who possesses the means to gratify every desire of your heart?

LUCY. A husband? Indeed, I never shall have a husband until Deloss returns from the war, and then I am to be married.

DOCTOR. Vat? You not marry me, ven dot is vat I coom for?

LUCY. If I am to be your wife, it will never be with my consent.

AUNT. [IMPERATIVELY.] Hush! Lucy. I have engaged our minister, and expect him here every moment.

LUCY. Indeed! Now I understand the purpose of all these preparations, this evening. I am to be forced to wed this man at once.

AUNT. Now, don't be foolish, Lucy. You are to be married to a wealthy gentleman, and that should give you joy.

LUCY. [DESPAIRINGLY.] Oh! Heavens! Is there no escape for me? Must I now bid adieu to all my bright visions of happiness with the only one I can ever love? Oh! misery! [Retreats in agitation.

AUNT. [GOING TO A DOOR.] Your uncle and the minister are here. Enter MR. LILLABRIDGE with the MINISTER. LUCY looks startled when seeing the MINISTER. The MINISTER greets MISS LUCY and MRS. LILLABRIDGE.

MINISTER. Am I too late?

AUNT. Just in time. [MR. LILLABRIDGE sits down. MRS. LILLABRIDGE introduces the DOCTOR to the MINISTER.

LUCY. It's a pity that I am no more allowed to answer for myself.

MINISTER. [TO DOCTOR.] Do you take Miss Lucy to be your wedded wife?

DOCTOR. Yes, sir, und to-tay too. [ALL IN ONE BREATH.] Mine profession ish a Toctor. I koon keep her foorst rate, too, mit mine profession.

ACT II.

CHARACTERS—1. MRS. LUCY PFEIFER. 3. THE DUTCH BAKER.
                    2. DOCTOR PFEIFER. 4 THE DUTCH BAKER'S WIFE.

SCENE I.—A SCENE IN A SHABBY KITCHEN.

MRS. LUCY PFEIFER is sitting at a table waiting for the DOCTOR'S appearance.

LUCY. I guess I'll call him. [OPENING A DOOR.] Doctor, your tea is ready. Come in.

DOCTOR enters, and places his hat in a chair. With a growl he seats himself at the table, resting his cane on his knees. LUCY pours him some tea.

LUCY. [GIVING HIM THE TEA.] Our tea is excellent this evening. Taste of it. [The DOCTOR, tasting of the tea, makes a disagreeable noise, pressing his lips together.

DOCTOR. [SHAKING HIS HEAD WITH ANGER.] Dot you call tea? Shlops I call dot, und nodding else. [SLAMS THE CUP DOWN.] Vere iss your rum in it? Oh! you fool you. You nefer put any rum in tot tea.   [LUCY acts frightened.

LUCY. [VERY CALM.] Why, Doctor, I never use such a thing. It makes people drunk. It surely must be a mistake. You cannot mean it.

DOCTOR. [ANGRILY.] You know nodding, you! You young shnips! You fool! You dry to dell me sometings? [LUCY PFEIFER, WITH FRIGHT, MOVES BACK HER CHAIR. THE DOCTOR, TAKING UP A PIECE OF A BREAD, TURNS IT OVER, THEN LOOKS CLOSELY AT IT IN AN ANGRY MANNER.—WITH A DEMONIACAL SNEER.] Vat? Preat? Preat you call tot? [SQEEZING IT IN THE FORM OF A BALL, HE SHOWS IT TO LUCY.] Dot shtuff you setted fore a shentlemans like me, und off mine profession? In der restaurant vere I ate mine tinner yesterday, I hat vat I call coot preat. It vas hart and paked so tot ven I ate it, it sounded like crackling nuts. Und dis stick in mine troat ven I eat him. Shame on yourself! [THROWING IT AT HER.] I shlam it ride trough your prains. Dot iss notting put raw toes.

Enter the DUTCH BAKER and WIFE.

LUCY. [WIPING HER EYES.] Come in. [DOCTOR runs up to them quickly with a piece of bread.

DOCTOR. [SHOWING IT TO THE BAKER.] Shust look here. Being you're der paker, I show you vat shtuff mine fife setted fore a shentlemans like me and off mine profession, to eat. You know I pe so peezy all tay mit mine profession, und ven I koom home she kifes me such sbtuff. [POINTING TO LUCY.] Dot ting don'd know nodding. [TO THE BAKER.] Did you efer see in our country such shtuff callt preat?

BAKER. [LOOKING AT IT.] Dot iss fery fine preat.

THE BAKER'S WIFE. Tot iss awful nice preat: so nice und raised so light. Dot iss finer as my man ken pake. You know, Doctor, fresh preat shtick himself so togetter ven she is varm. Yust set her out. Let her cool off a leedle vile und you hafe fery fine preat.

[LUCY weeps.

BAKER. [LOOKING AT LUCY, SAYS TO DOCTOR.] You must not pesh such a pat naans to tot young fife off yours. She get scart off you. She tincks all Dutchmans like us pe pat mens.

DOCTOR. I pesh a Sherman, not a Dutchman, sir. Und I pe Sherman py mine profession.

BAKER'S WIFE. [STROKING LUCY'S HAIR, SAYS TO DOCTOR.] See your poor vife. She pesh so vite. Vere are dose ret cheeks gone? [SHAKING HER HEAD.] You not keep her long. She iss notting for you pick rough Dutchmans. [DOCTOR ACTS ANGRY.—POINTING WITH HER FINGER.] You peesh Dutch, I peesh Dutch, und I ashame on you. You dreat dot voman so. [TO LUCY.—DOCTOR STILL ANGRY.] I tinck its petter you go home und shtay mit your Aunt who put you here to dot cross man. [WITH A WEEPING VOICE.] Oh, Godt! Dit you ask me vat he got, I toll you pooty quick notting. He got not vone cent off money.

DOCTOR. Who toll you?

BAKER'S WIFE. [POINTING TO DOCTOR.] You see dot fine watch chain, und dot fine shert, und dot plack coat, made fon dot finesten shtuff? Dot all pelongs to mine man. He married me in tem, und now he marry you, Lucy, in tem. Effery pody knows he porrowed tem from der paker.

DOCTOR. Who toll you dot?

BAKER'S WIFE. Who tell me tot? I tinck I ought to know who toll me tot. Vat I done know I'm sure you vont tell me.

THE BAKER. [ACTING SCARED.] You moost not dell all you know. Some dimes you Ret in droubles. Dot ish always der vay ven I toll you somedings. You dell always pefore mine face or pehint mine pack. [HARSHLY.] You pe shust like all der Americans vomans. Dey always dell efery ting.

BAKER'S WIFE. Vell, don't I dell der truth? He dit porrow tem from you.

DOCTOR. You pig liars. Vat for you tell dot to a man for off mine profession?

BAKER'S WIFE. Vell, kan't Doctors porrow shust as mooch as oter mans?

DOCTOR. [MENACINGLY.] Shame on you! I help you. Coming fore a man off mine—off mine profession, mit dot. [LEADING THEM TO THE DOOR.] I help you to come in mine house again. It's petter off you mine your peezness und I see to mine profession. I don't need you to dell vat you know. [Puts them out and closes the door.

SCENE II.—MRS. PFEIFER in a Private Room with her Infant.

MRS. PFEIFER. [SINGS.] Oh! land of rest, for thee I sigh.
    When will the moments come?
    When shall I lay my armor by,
        And dwell with thee at home?

Enter Baker's wife on tip-toe, with a bouquet of flowers.

BAKER'S WIFE. [WHISPERS AUDIBLY.] Oh! mine graciss. Vere iss der Toctor? Iss he mit himself zu house?

LUCY. No, come in.

BAKER'S WIFE. Oh! mine Godt. It iss awful zu tink apoud. I moost dells you dot ven der Toctor trowed mine man, der baker, oud fore der door, und oud off der house. You know mine man, der baker, he made himself so seek vile der Toctor shpeaked so base or mad off him, und now diss morning he lays in der bed, und I tought I vould run in trough der back door diss morning to dell you somedings apoud dat poor, proud Toctor Pfeifer, because he vears der baker's clothes, mit pants, coats und vest, und short, und hair vatch chain, mit golt shpeckles to go round tem. But now I must dell you vat iss der matter iss mit mine man. You know I can't shplain English very coot, but I dell you ven he vas put out off der toor by der Toctor, und I dell you it shtirred him all ofer up, und his gall proke, und proke him all ofer, und his liver is pad. Oh! Godt, Mrs. Pfeifer, I feel so mit you sorry; for shust tink vonce off your nice home vere you lived und you left, und den you coom to shtay mit dot cross man.

LUCY. Oh, yes indeed, he is so cruel, and I try to please him, yet he has only unkind words in store for me. Perhaps by kindness, which I always show towards him, I may make him a better man. At least, I pray that such may be the result. Oh, would you believe it? he does not even love this little child. Just think; last night he came home intoxicated, and ventured to strike this dear little darling, which is only three months old.

BAKER'S WIFE. Oh, Godt! Und you don't dell me dot. He shtrike dot little papy, und vat dit you do?

LUCY. Indeed, what could I do but walk with the sweet little pet in my arms for the rest of the night, and ask my Heavenly Father to forgive him and make him a better man? I do so much want him to love this little child and act as a father should.

BAKER'S W. Oh, grashus, Mrs. Pfeifer, mine mans ain't ugly off me, und off he vass, I shlamb der shticks off vood after him. I don'd pray to Godt for him, but den I feel for you awful sorry, und ven I knowed dot it maked der Toctor petter, I vould all der dime pray.

LUCY. Oh, dear woman. So much the more ought you to pray to God, thanking Him for giving you such a friend and companion. You don't know, or cannot comprehend, with what a rich gift you are blessed.

BAKER'S W. I forgot mincself. I moost dell you for vat for I coom in shust now to shpeak mit you. I vants to dell you all apoud dot vatch chain dot your man vears. Dot wery chain made off hair, mit der golt shpeckles arrount it. I vants to dell you dot hair vas vonce pelonging to der heat off mine man's motter vat iss deat. Vone dime pefore she vent to go deat, you know, she took der shaire und cut off her hair, und den she left her hair mit der hair-maker, und he maked der chain, und dot vas shoost pefore mine man took der pick shiff on der pick vater to coom off America. Dot you undershtand she done shoost vile ven she vass lifing yet, und shoost a leedle bit; und my, she cried mit her eyes vet, und told der baker you keep dot alvays. [PLEADINGLY.] Oh, Lucy, Lucy! von't you please got dot hair chain from der Toctor und gife it to me?

LUCY. I would gladly if I only could, but I dare not intercede for you. I think, however, that if you talk kindly to him in German, which he knows I can't understand, he will return the chain.

BAKER'S W. [TAPPING LUCY'S SHOULDER, SHOWS HER THE BOU-QUET.] Now I vill sing und dance for you like der beople in Hanover do dot iss near Holstein, ven dey go in der pick garten, und feel so goot like I do now, shust ven I know dot I get mine hair chain back, und you dells me sooch goot tings. [SINGS.]

Ein tag da ging ich in der Garten Schon und sahe dieses Blumchen weis;
Und ich fragte isr, ob sie liebte mich, und hats zu meinem Hertz gezwuugen.
Da ging ich zu dieses Feichlein hin, und sagte, ei wie Schon,
Und dan sie biegte ihre Kopf, und schaute in das Gras hinein.
Und als ich sahe Sie wahr ihm gefahr, da biegte ich ihre Kopf,
Und dan ich dachte, du bist so hübsch, und brach ab ihre Kopf.
    Tri, rie, ra, Tri, rie, ra,
    Du bist so schon.
    Tri, rie, ra, Trie, rie, ra, rie.

NOTE.—The song is to be sung in the air of the German waltz, "Lauderbach," or in that of "Where, oh, where is my little dog gone?" When singing, " tri, rie, ra," and waltzing the German, which should be done in good character, she flies off one of her slippers across the stage, then picks it up and waves it over her head, deftly taking off the other one, and waltzing without the slippers in a lively manner.

Dis iss der vay to pe heppy. Dance und sing like you see der Dutch woman do like me. Und von dot pat Doctor off yours coom home, take a shtool und knock him oud off der door und house, mit der shtool over his head, und den he'll have reshpect for you. Dot iss der vay ve Sharman voman make it.

LUCY. Oh, no. That would indeed be wrong. I never could lay hands on him nor strike him with anything.

BAKER'S W. Vell you see he shtrike you, und I pet ven he shtrike you von dime you shoost shtrike him pack six dimes, und I pet he not shtrike you any more so quick, und ven he shtrike you again und iss so pad, you coom und shtay py me und der baker. Ve like you. You pe so coot, und ve make it so coot py you.

Enter Dutch Baker.

DUTCH BAKER. Vife, vife, you gife me von terrible shcare. You shtay from me so long avay.

BAKER'S W. I vent first in der garden.

BAKER. You shtayed so long avay.

BAKER'S W. I vass all right. I yoost danze und sing. I pe awful happy. [PITYINGLY.] Oh, see poor Lucy. She feels so pad, und I sing und danzed for her. [HURRIEDLY.] Coom, now ve sing und danze a Dutchlander valtzer, vat ve sing in Sharmany, apoud der King, ven ve get free, und don'd vant any more King, but vant ein Bresident, like ve got in America.

BAKER. [COUGHS.] I not can sing any. Mine liver iss so pad since der Toctor put me oud off der house. [Coughs.

BAKER'S W. [TAKES THE BAKER BY THE HANDS.] It makes nodding oud. I sing und you shust shtep mit me.

[SINGS.] 　　　　Boomps foll dra,
　　　　Brauchen keine Konig mehr,
　　　　Boomps foll dra.
　　　　Boomps foll dra,
　　　　Brauchen keine Konig mehr,
　　　　Boomps foll dra.
　　　In dieses Land, wier brauchen keine Konig mehr,
　　　　Boomps foll dra, etc.

[The air is waltz time. After concluding the song the baker's wife looks out of the door saying, hurriedly:

When she sings the word " Blumchen," in the first verse, she bows to LUCY and points out the white flower which she holds in the other hand. When she sings the words, "Hertz gezwungen," she presses the bouquet to her heart and pauses before reversing and singing the second verse. When singing the second verse, the word " Feichlein" refers to a violet in the bouquet, which she also points out to LUCY with a bow, and then proceeds with dancing and singing. At the end of the chorus she gives the bouquet to LUCY, which is graciously accepted.

Der Toctor iss cooming zu home. I moost go to my house so dot he
not see me. Dot pad Toctor.   [Departs.

Enter DOCTOR PFEIFER.

DOCTOR, [To LUCY.] Vat are you doing here mit der baker?
You young shnips! You make love to otter mens, und sing und dance
mit dem ven I'm not to home?

LUCY. [SIGHS.] Oh, dear, what next?

BAKER. [EXCITED.] Be not so mad, Toctor. I never danzed
vonce in all mine life. Ven I vas living I never danzed mit your vife.
You tink sooch a vooman as she danze, ven she coon dell all apoud
Heaven und der angels? Look at her. You tink she look like danz-
ing?

DOCTOR. [To LUCY.] Didn't I hear you shtep, und don'd you
dare to tell me no?

LUCY. Oh, no, Doctor, you are wrong. It was the baker and his
wife that you heard dancing. I aspire to something different. I have
done nothing wrong or out of place. Have I not often told you that
people who are not true to themselves are never true to others? And
those who are untrue to themselves are surely never true to their
God.

DOCTOR. Vat? Vat you say? You say und toll me again dot I
vear anoter man's clothes?

LUCY. You don't understand me.

DOCTOR. Shtop your noise! I show you pooty quick off I under-
shtant you or not, und don'd you dare to shpeak to me anoter vord
until I dell you to.

LUCY. I am always trying to do right, yet never please. Oh! I
am indeed a wronged orphan.

DOCTOR. [To BAKER.] Didn't I toll you dot dime ven I putted
you und your vife oud off der door dot you should shtay dare, outside off der door, und never coomt in mine house vonce more?

BAKER. Yes, you toll me dot, but I tought I come vonce more,
und ask you like a man to gife me up my deat motter's hair mit in der
watch chain. Coat, pants und otter tings you pe velcome to, und I
shpeck nodding more off dot. Now give me up dot deat motter's off
mine hair chain.

DOCTOR. [TAKES OFF THE CHAIN AND THROWS IT AT THE BAKER.]
Shtep mit yourself out der toor, und I pe a man vat coom fon Hanover, vere I learned to be a Toctor, und you not insult after diss tay a
man like me in mine profession any more.

BAKER. [GOING TO THE DOOR WITH THE CHAIN.] Oh, Lucy, I
moost shoost say vone vord before I leave, und dot iss, der Toctor
hat in Sharmany a girl one, two, three, four years, und den you see
he did not show his big humbug papers off his to her, mit dose big
gounselmans' names on dem, und der big zeals fon wax mit red und
black colors. Done you know, dey all know him over dare? I dells
you somedimes vat dose bapers are. Dose pe bapers vat he shtole

from hiss uncle. Hiss uncle iss a bick officer, und vears dose bick tings on his shoulders. Hiss uncle pe py der King an officer in Sharmany. He shtole dem from his uncle Heinrich, und den coom off America, und made you und your aunt pelieve dot dey pe so coot as so much golt. Good for notting dey pe. Humbug shtuff dey pe in America.

Doctor. [Striking the floor with his cane.] You good for notting, you coom in mine house und shpeak love to mine vife.

Baker. Good py, Lucy! I dell you more somedimes.

Lucy. Never mind; I know it all.   [The baker departs.

Doctor. Vill you co oud to der coal pits und tend to dem, or I kill you. Und vill you rake up der leaves und coal. You lazy ting you. You ken too dot. Off you don'd hafe dot tone py der dime I kets home I kill you. You undershtand dot? Und you pring in der vood for der stofes, und der vater. Dot iss your blase. You tinck a man off mine profession does such vork? Your der voman, und it's your blase. I don'd vant to soil mine hants for a man off mine profession. You shnuffer you! Shtanding rount here, shnuffing unt crying all tay.

Lucy. [Weeping.] Oh, Doctor, please do not feel so hard towards me. Please remember, I am only a young girl, and unused to labor. Do not be angry, please. I shall do all that I can. I'll go to the coal pits.

Doctor. Shut your mout! Co to dot Irish Jim, our hired man. He dells you pooty quick vat to do, und ven your work iss tone I talk please mit you den. Hoory up pefore der storm commences.

[Doctor and Lucy depart.

ACT III.

SCENE I.—Among the Coal Pits.

Characters—1. Mrs. Lucy Pfeifer   2. Irish Jim.
and Infant.

Enter Irish Jim—rakes coal. Enter Mrs. Lucy Pfeifer with her infant on her back and a Bible in her hand. Jim stops raking. The winds howl.

Mrs. Pfeifer. Please tell me what to do. Doctor Pfeifer sent me to ask you about tending these coal pits.

Jim. Oh! En yer dear crathur. En vhat are yer after doin' in this ere place?. [The winds howl.] En in this fearful storm thet's raging? [Looking at her dress.] With yer clothes froze clear above yer knees, sure? En faith,'an' ye will die with that ere young un on yer back. [Lucy weeps.] Yez will nivir git back to yer house agin alive. [Jim leaning on the rake meditates.] En it's you thet's sick en will be froze ter death here.

[The thunder rolls and the winds rage. JIM pulls down his
 ear-laps. LUCY spreads out a shawl on the snow-
 bank and sits down.

LUCY. I would gladly die were it only possible. Life is only a
burden to me.

JIM. En did the Docthor sind yez down here, thinkin' thet yer
could do the haulin' uv this ere black coal with thet ere child upon
yer back, wich is only three months old, jist? [STORM CONTINUES.]
Do yez know yer ought ter be in bid, and not here in sich a storm?

LUCY. Oh! Jim, I can't help it! I am only a sold orphan. My
earthly happiness was sacrificed by my unnatural aunt, and now all
that remains for me to do is to bear my burden of wrong with Christian resignation. [OPENS HER BIBLE.] Do you ever read the Bible?
You believe there is a Christ who sees all we do, both the good and
the evil, do you not? I know this Bible is my only guide through life.

JIM. [NODDING HIS HEAD.] En faith, an' I believe it all. I ken
not read the Bible meself, but I believe it all. I niver heard any uv
the likes uv it though, but then I believe it onyhow.

LUCY. Well, Jim, I shall read a few verses, and then go to work.
                                   [She reads from Matt. ii., 28, 29.

JIM. Amen!

LUCY. You see, Jim, where it is written, "Come unto me, all that
labor and are heavy laden, and I will give thee rest," It means if we
believe in Him and are troubled, and we go to Him in prayer, He will
comfort us and give us rest.

JIM. [CLAPS HIS HANDS AND DROPS THE RAKE.] Ah, ah! En faith,
me dear lady, en its rest thet I've bin afther this long time. En if I'll
git it jist for the askin' uv it, you bet, en I'll be afther askin' Him.
En it's the divil the bit uv coals thet I'll be rakin' any more. Ah! en
I'll be askin' Him right away.

LUCY. Why, Jim, you did not understand me. That isn't the
way. If you worked no more, what would you have to eat?

JIM. Ha, ha! I don't want anything to ate, it's rest thet I'm afther. [TAKING LUCY BY THE ARM.] En, me dear crathur, arise from
yer sittin'. May the Lard kape yez from harrum an' protect ye. En
may yer life be as aisy as it has bin hard before. En the Lard be me
jedge, ye shall not work a minnit here to-day. It's very tadjeus, an'
I ken not do very much meself, but by workin' the half uv an hour I
kin do more then a weak woman in the half uv a day. [LEADING HER
BY THE ARM.] Come on, an' I'll be afther seein' yer safe to yer home.
En then, afther seein' yer safe to yer home, I'll be afther askin' Jaisus
to be givin' yer a rest an' meself too. Opon me word, ye shall not
work to-day.   [Both depart.

ACT IV.

CHARACTERS.—1 DR. PFEIFER.   3. IRISH JIM.
         2. FIVE PATIENTS.   4. LUCY AND INFANT.

SCENE I.—THE DOCTOR IN HIS OFFICE READING.

Enter FELIX, with a handkerchief around his face; MIKE, with a
    disabled foot, (appears ridiculous;) CRAWFORD, with a sore
    throat; A PEASANT, holding his side and coughing; A GEN-
    TEEL LOOKING GENTLEMAN, with a bandaged arm.

[The DOCTOR, seeing his patients all enter at once, looks bewil-
    dered. After talking in a low tone with each one, he gives
    him a chair, and then begins to take the bandage off the pa-
    tient's arm. A cry is heard from each patient, " 'Tend to me
    first." " Doctor, I can't wait." " Mine hurts the most."
    "Pull my tooth." The DOCTOR puts some medicine in the
    tooth. " Have you time to give me medicine?" is heard from
    the man who coughs.

DOCTOR. Now, shentlemens, as you all coomt in mine office on
der same time, I can't vait on you all. Dis iss mine profession, und I
see to you ven I get rount to you. [TAKING THE BANDAGE OFF.]
Dis man has to open his store und see to his profession, so I 'tend to
him first.

MIKE. [SHOUTS.] Oh! I wish e'd eh got on me collar end Sunday
clothes, then maybe ye'd a seen to me first.

FELIX. [HAS THE TOOTHACHE.] Doctor, I consider I'm yust as
coot und know yust as mooch as dot man mit der vine clothes.

DOCTOR. You're mistaken. I don't tink nodding off dot kint.
It is his profession. Und he vants to see to his profession, und in
yours you don't be in such a hoory.

Enter LUCY with her infant on her back, and wet clothes, return-
    ing from the coal pits. DOCTOR acts frightened, and pre-
    tends that she is a beggar woman.

DOCTOR. Shame on you! You olt becker, mit your young vone
on your pack. Vat you mean—coming in a Doctor's office, mit your
clothes all frose ice und vet, und fore a shentleman off mine profession? Go from mine office! Be off mit you. [PUSHING HER OUT OF
THE DOOR.] Shtay dare and ket dry. [TO PATIENTS.] Der darnet
beckers always podder mine office so.   [DOCTOR resumes dressing
                                      the arm.

A PATIENT. Doctor, where is your young wife?

DOCTOR. She iss kone to fisit some frients.

Enter IRISH JIM.

DOCTOR. [FRIGHTENED,] Vat you vant? I tought you vas mit
mine vife tenting der coal pits. Mine your peesness. Co oud.

JIM. In Hivin's name! You're the Doctor. It is I thet brought yer wife end child through the starm. I nivir will ask yez a cint for doin' the rakin' uv thet air coal an' leaves. An' don't yer iver send yer wife an' child out there agin.

DOCTOR. [INTERRUPTING.] It vas a becker. Shut up! She ain't mine vife. You tinck a man in mine profession like me sent mine vife in der coal pits?

JIM. En didn't I hear yer tell when I woos by the door listenin' thet she'd gone to see her friends?

DOCTOR. [WITH GUILT.] Shut up. Moost you dell all you know pefore volks?

JIM. For all yez the Docthor. I'll tell yez agin, that poor crathur kin nivir shtand the slave wark thot yer a givin' her to do.

[The DOCTOR flings a bottle at JIM.

DOCTOR. Vat you mean? Don'd you know notting? Comin' on pefore mine batients und insulting mine profession. Comin' mit such shtuff, und delling pefore mine patients. Co to der hot blace, you Irishman you! You fool mit such talk. Co in der hot blace!

JIM. En, Doctor, on whet are yer mad for?

DOCTOR. [SHAKING HIS FIST.] I show you pooty quick vat for. You insult me und mine profession? I dell you git oud off mine office! '[JIM leaving, looks back at every step. The DOCTOR with a trembling hand pours something from a bottle on the broken arm. With his greatest efforts he tries to not pour it on the floor, but all in vain; his hands are both too unsteady.

A PATIENT. Doctor, sit down; then your arm won't tremble.

DOCTOR. Oh, dot darned old becker voman, mit dot young vone on her pack, upsetted me completely. I can't do nodding any more. Dey alvays drouble mine office so.' Der eferlasting beckers. You vait once. I see Lucy Pfeifer to-night.

[The DOCTOR trying to sit on a chair, sits with excitement on the floor. Upon rising to pour medicine on the arm he drops the bottle.

SCENE II.—DOCTOR PFEIFER'S OFFICE.

CHARACTERS—1. DR. PFEIFER.   2. CHARLES ROWELL.
          3. LUCY PFEIFER.

The DOCTOR is discovered compounding medicine. Enter
CHARLES ROWELL.

DOCTOR. [RISING QUICKLY.] Vat you vant? Vat can I do for you to-tay?

CHARLES. Are you Doctor Pfeifer?

DOCTOR. [RUBBING HIS HANDS.] Yes, I'm Doctor Pfeifer. Who dit you shpose I vas? Vat coon I do for you? Vat you vant?

CHARLES. I am Charles Rowell. Your wife and my mother are old friends.

DOCTOR. Vat? Your fotter iss an old frient off mine vife?

CHARLES. Oh, no. My father died long years ago. It is my mother who is well acquainted with your wife.

DOCTOR. Vat dit your motter vant off mine vife?

CHARLES. Nothing, only my mother would like to renew her acquaintance.

DOCTOR. No, sir. My vife iss peesy. You can't see mine vife. She hass got a blenty off otter peezness mittout talking mit strangers.

CHARLES. Beg pardon, Doctor. You misunderstand me.

DOCTOR. Vat? Vat for you vant a partner? You vant to go in partnership mit mine vife?

CHARLES. You don't understaud me yet. I have called to see if you wish to have a student to study medicine with you. I would like to be a doctor some day.

DOCTOR. Oh! it's mine profession dot you vaut to learn. Now I undershtand you. You knows somedings apoud medicine?

CHARLES. Yes, sir. I have been six months steady in a drug store. I thought I could learn from you when I heard that you had studied in the old country, and that you are a master of the German language.

DOCTOR. Mashter off mine profession? You shoost bet. I mashter him every time, und I don't vant anypody to do it for me eeter.

CHARLES. Yes, I understand you are kept very busy.

DOCTOR. Yes, sir. If you vas here in mine office yesterday, und you hat seen all mine patients vas here, you vouldn't vonder. I knew not vich von to look to last otter first.

CHARLES. Do you think you would like to have any one assist you in your office, and read with you?

DOCTOR. Reat mit me? Done you tink I coon reat mine books alone mittout your help? I tinks you done know pooty mooch apoud der Sharmans.

CHARLES. I presume I don't. This is my first experience with a German. My mother is an American.

DOCTOR. Vat? Iss your motter an Afrairican voman? [LAUGHS.] Vell, vell, I done vonder any dot you hafe to look to der Sharmans for to get 'sperience. Yoost vait vonce. I hafe got an Afrairican vife, und efery time dot I got anytiug mit her to sav she completely upsetted me. Der Afrairicans nefer undershtand tings right, und dey nefer dell tings as dey ought to be tole. Done you tink dot der Afrairican vomans are funny? Dare iss mine vife, she tole me von tay dot a man shoot a bear, und der next day she tole me dot der man kilt der bear. Dey nefer tole tings as dey ought to be tole, so dat you undershtand dem right avay quick. Anoter dime, take it for instance ven you read der newspaper in America, dey hafe it von tay dat Mishter

So-und-so iss tead, und der next tay, ven you look on der newspaper, dey say he iss a nice man. So, vat you shall tink?

CHARLES. In that case I don't know.

DOCTOR. I tink it iss a first class hoombug. I tink it's better dey should not be toleing vat dey done know.

CHARLES. I think so myself, but what is your decision? Do you want me to be your student?

DOCTOR. [GIVING HIM A CHAIR.] Sit down on der chair und I shpeak mit you after a vile. [DEPARTS TO GET CIGARS—RETURNS AND PROFFERS THEM.] Hafe a shmoke mit me. Dose be fine Havaners.

CHARLES. Thank you, Doctor, I never indulge.

DOCTOR. Oh, yes, sir, yes. Shmoking iss allowed in mine office. You may pe intulged. You see I shtick some fire on mine, und you see I shmoke right avay.

CHARLES. You misunderstand me. I never smoke or use tobacco in any form.

DOCTOR. Vat? You say dose cigars be der common forms? I gife you to undershtand dose are der pest Havaners cigars, und efery von costed me ten cents, und done you know dose are not de common forms, und efery cigar grows alike.

CHARLES. Thank you. I don't use tobacco in any form.

DOCTOR. Take von, I tole you. Dey done grow on mine farm. Dey grow down in Havaner, shoost like you see dem, und efery von costed me five cents on a hundert to get dem up here. Dey grow in Havaner, und dot's vere dey deprived deir name. Der transmittance costed me five cents on der hundert.

CHARLES. Excuse me. It makes me sick to smoke.

DOCTOR. Vell, vell. You done shmoke, und den you vant to learn mine profession? How you tink you efer learn to pe a Toctor py profession von you done nefer learn to shmoke? Dot iss der vay to learn to pe a shentleman. Take your cigar und chewing tobacco, und leaf der Americans' temperance alone, und go oud among shentlemen.

CHARLES. I never care to be one.

DOCTOR. Vell, coom ofer der shtreet, und ve go to see Mishter Moshneritz' saloon, und off you done shmoke, und vant to shtop mit me, coom hafe a glass beer.

CHARLES. Oh, no. Oh, no, indeed. I never drink beer or any other spirits.

DOCTOR. Vat? You done vant to take a glass beer, und den vant to shtop mit me und mine office?

CHARLES. You will have to excuse me from such things. It would grieve my mother too much. I think I am capable of learning all that your books in the library contain without drinking or smoking.

DOCTOR. Vell, vell. You sit still dare until I coom pack. I feel so pad in mine heat, so dot I feel shoost like I could drink a glass beer.   [Departs.

Enter LUCY.

LUCY. Oh! Charlie Rowell, how do you do? How is your mother? When I was in the library, a few moments ago, I thought I recognized your voice, but was not certain.

CHARLES. . My mother is very well, and sends you her love. I called to see your husband about studying medicine with him.

LUCY. Indeed. Did you make an engagement with the Doctor?

CHARLES. No, not yet. He doesn't seem to understand English very well, and is quite excitable. He has just gone out to get a glass of beer.

LUCY. Well, Charlie, I am very to sorry to say it, but I think you and Doctor Pfeifer could never agree together. He is so very peculiar in his ways, and so persistent in carrying out his own ideas that you would find your association with him very trying indeed.

CHARLES. Still, if I fail to effect an arrangement with the Doctor, it will be a disappointment to my mother, as she thought it would be pleasant for me to spend my time here, on account of your friendship for her.

LUCY. It would be very pleasant indeed; that is, if you could agree with the Doctor. I feel certain that you could not. He understands but little of English, and worse still, he will allow no one to explain it to him. It is so very embarrassing to have him misunderstand you.

CHARLES. The Doctor always seems to be very busy.

LUCY. Yes He is nearly all of the time absent from home, but I seldom know where he is.

CHARLES. Is that possible? You—his wife—in ignorance of his whereabouts when absent from home?

LUCY. He deems me too young to be informed respecting his movements, and if I venture to question him concerning them, it is certain to call forth a rebuff from him.

CHARLES. Indeed. It must be exceedingly unpleasant for you.

LUCY. Yes. I hardly know how to appear when in his presence. I often wonder, Charlie, if my dear mother, when dying, knew that my life would be so hard a struggle. I well remember that she placed her hand upon my head and bade me always do right.

CHARLES. I don't think she knew anything about it. It was all the work of your unnatural aunt.

Enter DOCTOR.

DOCTOR. [ANGRY.] Halloo, Lucy! Vat you do, shtanding rount here unt talkit mit strangers?

LUCY. No, no, Doctor, he is no stranger. I have known him since he was a little boy. His mother and I are the best of friends.

DOCTOR. Dot iss a pooty shtory to dell me. Ven I valk shoost now in der house, und catched you shtanding und talking low mit him dare. I tought I tole you so often to not valk in mine office mitout mine permission from me. Done I hear you dell him shoost now dot you go und lif mit him und his motter? Und you not shtay by me? You young shnips. Iss dot der vay you talk on shtrangers ven you tink I done look on you?

LUCY. I haven't said anything out of place.

DOCTOR. [TAKING HOLD OF LUCY'S ARM.] Vill you tole me quick vat you tole dot shtrange young man?

LUCY. Yes. I was talking about my dead mother, and about his studying with you.

DOCTOR. [BOWING.] Yes, yes. Dot iss all very fine for you to talk. [POINTING AT THE DOOR.] Vill you valk mit yourself oud mine office? Done you be toleing nodding any more.

LUCY. Mrs. Fairwood wants you to call and see her sick child.
[Departs.

DOCTOR. [SHOUTS.] It's you I vant to see apoud, und not otter folks' sick shilds.

CHARLES. Have you decided what answer I shall give my mother?

DOCTOR. Vat you tink I got to do mit vat you tole your motter? I shpose off she iss a frient off mine vife, she sing to you all tay long apoud der templeranclers und der cold vaters all der dime. I see by your not shmoking a fine Havaner cigar, vat grows in Havaner shoost as you see dem, your motter iss all der dime preaching der templeranclers to you, shoost like mine vife.

CHARLES. Yes, my mother is strictly a temperance woman.

DOCTOR. Vat you tink I do mit you in mine office, ven you von't make yourself a shentleman among shentlemen? You vant to do, young man, as a shentleman ought to do. Dot is, you take your Havaner cigar und your brandy-vine und your glass beer. How you expect to got your lifing ven you von't do as shentlemen ought to? For exsample: Ven a man asks you, "You hafe a cigar?" und you say, "I shmoke not;" ven dey ask you, "You take a glass beer?" you say, "I trink notting;" you make a fine shtudent, done you, for a man to be in mine profession? Done I tole you dot iss so comish, ven a young voman, man, shild or boy, speaks frients mit mine vife, dey all bellefe in der cold vaters, und der sing-song choress off der temperance. I tink it's petter, young man, off you go a leedle longer off school, until you learn to shpell und undershtand ven folks shpeak shtreight mit you; und you petter learn to trink your beer like a shentleman, und shmoke a fine Havaner cigar, den you can coom diss vay vonce more. After you hafe forgot und you not tink any more off your temperance, you might coom und I shpeak shtudent mit you den.

CHARLES [WIPES PERSPIRATION FROM HIS FACE.] How long, Doctor, do you think it will take me to accomplish all this?

DOCTOR. I tink off you pe pooty shmart, in apoud fife years you learn it all. Und vat you tink you do in mine office off you didn't know how to shpell goot? I hafe sooch great bick Latin pooks, mit great pick Sharman letters. It iss more as you coult do to get troo der toor mit von und lift him. Some of mine pooks are a half off an inch tick, und how you shpect you get tem fixed in your heat? Dose Toctor pooks dells us mit blain talk all apoud der shtructure off der human system off der human frame. Dot means der excel-letton. You know vat der excel-letton iss, done you? Dot iss vat iss left after you insect dem, und vat iss left after you poot der poddies avay und bickle dem, und nodding shtays goot poot der pones, vat off Sharman iss called "kenochon." You hafe to be pe pooty shmart, young man, in order to get so far as to go off an academy, vich off English means a school. I hafe peen all trough der school, und vass called a pooty shmart poy pecause I hat to go pack der second dime, und didn't pass exsamination ven der otters did. I had to pegin ofer again pefore I got mine bapers. Dot vass pecause I vass so faraheat off der otters. You couldn't tole py mine lankguage mit peoples dot I ofer hafe peen off school and trough a academy to learn mine profession? I tinks I am a very ordinary shentleman, und don'd prag apoud mineself to beoples, und I valk mit mineself pooty shtrate.

CHARLES. I think you are very extra-ordinary. [TAKES A LETTER FROM HIS POCKET.] I would like to give this letter to Mrs. Pfeifer. It is from my mother.

DOCTOR. [EXCITEDLY BRUSHES HIS HAIR.] Hem! hem! Mine Godt! Mine grashus! Gife me dot letter. I gife it to her mineself. It's from your fotter, iss it? [CHARLES places the letter back in his pocket.

DOCTOR. [TAKES HIM BY THE ARM.] Young man, young man, vill you dell me pooty quick how long dot you talked mit mine vife und vile I vas gone? Gife me dot letter.

CHARLES. I shall give it back to my mother, and tell her that she had better see Mrs. Pfeifer personally, as you and I don't seem to understand each other.

DOCTOR. Vot for hass your fotter got to coom? Done I tole you dot I pet you he nefer vill shpeak mit mine Lucy? I preak mit mine cane hiss heat. You pet, after diss mine vife nefer vill coom in mine office so quick again. [OPENS THE DOOR.] You valk oud. You shtep mit yourself oud. [CHARLES REMAINS STANDING.] You dell your fotter I tink it's petter dot he nefer cooms near mine office. He vill nefer coom to shpeak mit mine Lucy Pfeifer, or I get mine involver und shoot him tead.

CHARLES. You are so forgetful. How can my poor father come when he died a long time ago? You get mad about nothing, I see. I am sorry if I have occasioned your wife to have unkindness shown her. She does not deserve it, Doctor.

DOCTOR. [POINTING TO THE DOOR.] Make mit yourself oud. I help you. Telling me dot you make off me persefes. I shpose dot to-day you Afrairican tole dot you shoot a bear trough der ear, und to-morrow you tole dot you killed him. I tole you vonce so often dot ven I hafe anotter shtudent dot I get a Sharman poy vot hass hiss prains togetter. [Depart CHARLES, forgetting his hat, which the DOCTOR throws at him out of the door.

CHARLES. [SHOUTS OUTSIDE.] I guess I'll never call again, Doctor. When the five years are up I'll remember my experience with you.

ACT V.

SCENE I.—A MILLINER SHOP.

CHARACTERS—1. MRS. LUCY PFEIFER.   3. THE LITTLE CHILD.
2. TWO SHOP GIRLS.   4. DR. PFEIFER.
5. AUNTIE FLAGAN.

Enter LUCY and MILLIE.

LUCY. What did that lady want yesterday?

MILLIE. [SEWING ON A HAT.] She wanted blue ribbons and a spray of forget-me-nots. She left the face trimming for you to decide.

Enter a shop girl with the little child, and DR. PFEIFER carrying two cucumbers.

DOCTOR. [SHOUTING.] Halloo dare! See, I cot two coocumbers. I vant mine tinner.

MRS. PFEIFER. [TRIMMING HURRIEDLY.] Why, Doctor, it is only ten o'clock.

DOCTOR. It makes no tifferance. You tinck a shentleman like me und off mine profession must shlave und shtarfe six dimes a tay? [ANGRILY.] Pring me on der winiger. I vant to fix dose coocumbers for mine self.

LUCY. Please take the baby from Mary, papa, then I shall send her over to the store to get some vinegar.

DOCTOR. Vat you! Vat in hell! [FLINGS THE CUCUMBERS AT HER.] Vat, no winiger in dis house? I help you mit your please. Vat kint off a housekeeper you pe? [CHILD CRIES WITH FRIGHT.] Shtop dot young vone's mout, or I knock her tead.

LUCY. [TAKING THE CHILD.] Please, papa, don't frighten baby. I am going to get the vinegar myself. Come, Mamie, go by-by with mama.

DOCTOR. Yes, I py-py paby you. Dot is alvays der vey in dis house, ven I vant somedings to eat. La, la, ish der vay efery ting goes in dis house, und for a man off mine profession.

[The DOCTOR enraged flings the bonnets one after another from the racks, then stamps on them. He then pounds the table with his fist.

DOCTOR. I help you mit la, la, und bonnets.

[The girls run screaming from the shop. The DOCTOR chases his wife and child to the door, and then strikes at her with an open knife, and she falls screaming in the doorway.

DOCTOR. [KICKING HER.] You common street ting you! I kill you mit dot cross childs! I send you poth to der tefil!

LUCY. [SCREAMING.] Oh, my neck!

Enter AUNTIE FLAGAN, stepping over LUCY.

AUNTIE FLAGAN. [WITH CLASPED HANDS.] Ah! en the Lard Almighty. En is she did? Th' dair crathur. [BENDING LUCY'S HEAD.] En faith, en she's did, Docthor.   [She seats the child in a chair.

AUNTIE F. Quick, Docthor! Liff her up with me en take her to the bid. [THEY TAKE HER TO A BED.—SHAKING LUCY'S NECK.] En faith, Docthor, you finished her this time. En it's her thet's did. [CRYING.] Oh, the dair crathur.

DOCTOR. You pesh right, Mrs. Flagan. She is a crasy screecher. She screeches shust to see how many more she can set crasy, shust like herself.

AUNTIE F. Oh, but her neck is broke.

DOCTOR. [EXAMINING LUCY'S HEAD.] Her heat lasts yet, und pesh coot for dis many years yet. She shust proke her neck, dot's all.

AUNTIE F. En sure, Docthor, I think thet's enough.

DOCTOR. Quick, pring me a powl. I quick pring her ond off her crasy fits und screeching. I pleet her arm. Dot ve to mit all crasy folks. [MRS. F. brings the DOCTOR a bowl. He bleeds his wife's arm.

Two angels robed in white appear among clouds, and with outstretched wings flutter over LUCY.

LUCY. [WITH A FAINT VOICE.] Do you hear [RISES] the angels sing? Will the angels come to me. How nice the angels' harp plays. [SINKING LOW IN HER BED.] How sweet the sounds are.

[The DOCTOR drops the bowl at hearing this.

AUNTY F. En sure, Doctor, th' good angels hiv got her this time. Sure, en she's as white as the angels above her.   [Angels disappear.

LUCY. [LEANING ON THE PILLOW, RAISING HER HEAD.] Oh, Auntie, why did you bring me back? Didn't you hear the angels sing?

[Closing her eyes and resting her head faintly on the pillow.

DOCTOR. [SHAKING HIS WIFE'S ARM AND PEERING IN HER FACE.] Vake up here, Lucy. [HOLDING THE BABY OVER HER.] Your papy is crying und vants you, Lucy. Lucy! Lucy Pfeifer! Vake up dare!

[A white dove flies in.

AUNTIE FLAGAN. En sure! en thet's a good sign. The angels and doves claim her. En didn't I always tell yer, Doctor, thet she woos always too good for this ere world?   [The dove flies away.

LUCY. Oh, Doctor! If you wish to kill me, you can do so; but first send our little child to Mrs. Woods, and she will know what to do. Do that in Heaven's name. It is all I ask.

DOCTOR. [ANGRY.—TO AUNTIE F.] Shust hear her vonce, how crasy she talks. You tinck I kill mine vife, hay?

AUNTIE F. Ye must take good care uv her, or she'll die. She's sich a frail crathur. [A black hawk flies in and picks at the DOCTOR.

AUNTIE F., frightened, takes the child from the DOCTOR, who almost lets it fall.

DOCTOR. Oh, Godt! Oh, Godt! Mrs. Flagan, I tidn't tinck mine vife pe so pad. I shust tought I shtir her up a leedle, shust to make her vork petter. [The hawk, picking at the DOCTOR's face, makes him fall fainting to the floor. DOCTOR rises and knocks the hawk's head off against the wall, exclaiming: "Dare, you plack rascal! You not sheare anoter man off mine profession like dot!"

SCENE II.—THE MILLINER SHOP. LUCY AND SHOP GIRLS ARE DISCOVERED TRIMMING BONNETS.

Enter MRS. LILLABRIDGE.

LUCY. What can I do for you? Would you like to see some hats?

MRS. LILLABRIDGE. [REMOVES HER VEIL.] Don't you know me?

LUCY. Oh! it's you—Auntie Lillabridge.

AUNT. Oh! my dear darling Lucy, you are so changed. I never should have recognized you as being my little blue-eyed darling of long ago.

LUCY. Oh, do not repeat darling to me again. It calls to memory my happy childhood days. I am nobody's darling now. There is no one to love me but God. I am alone with Him. He takes me gently by the hand and leads me through all the dark and rough ways of my life.

AUNT. [EMBRACES LUCY.] Where is your husband?

LUCY. Husband? I have no husband. I am a lonely orphan, forced to battle with life unaided, and full of sorrow. My property has been squandered by the drunken, worthless object to whom you sold me. He neither fears God nor respects man. Did I not tell you once, Auntie, that I was no tamer of lions? He curses me for every good act that I perform, accuses me of wrong where none is done, and ill-treats me on every occasion. My burden is indeed heavier than I can bear, and I am often unable to care for my dear children.

AUNT. [WITH SURPRISE.] You have children?

LUCY. Yes, I have two little light-haired children.

AUNT. And doesn't Doctor Pfeiffer care for or support his children?

LUCY. No, indeed. He cares for no one but the saloon keeper.

AUNT. My poor Lucy. Will you now return home with me? I have come for the purpose of having you part from Doctor Pfeifer, with whom you can leave the children. Then you shall be my pet Lucy once more.

LUCY. Oh! Auntie, do you think that the offer of a palace home would for one moment tempt me to desert my dear little children, and leave them in the care of their inhuman father? No. Where I go, my children must follow. Nothing but death shall ever separate me from them, until they are old enough to care for themselves. All of this torture and sorrow you alone brought upon me. Yet I shall not reproach you for it. I shall as freely forgive you as I hope to be forgiven; but oh! Auntie, promise me that you never will again be guilty of selling a human soul. Let not the glitter of gold so dazzle and blind your eyes as to lead you to another folly like this.

AUNT. Then you refuse to return to the home of your childhood?

LUCY. Yes, unless you would permit my children to accompany me. If you consent to that, I will willingly be your kitchen girl.

AUNT. What? You become my menial?

LUCY. Do think that would be harder or more degrading than to wash all day with an infant tied to my back, or to be driven to attend coal pits in a freezing storm? My common task has been to drudge all day and sew at night with a babe in my arms, without daring to murmur.

AUNT. Why did you obey that inhuman wretch?

LUCY. Could I do otherwise? This, dear Auntie, is the result of your selling me to your so-called cultured and rich European physician. Weren't you unfeeling and inhuman to act as covertly as you did in betraying me into that man's hands?

AUNT. Lucy, you are too severe. I, also, was deceived in the Doctor. Why did you not part?

LUCY. I would have left him, had I not been afraid of the uncharitable comments that would have followed my flight. I could not face the scorn of the world, sure to be visited upon my head, for, as you are aware, very few knew of the artful manner in which you had entrapped me into that unholy marriage.

AUNT. Oh! Lucy, Lucy, pardon me. Forget it all, and return home. Disappointment and remorse of conscience overwhelm me since learning how basely the Doctor deceived us both. Once more I ask you to accept my offer. Why not leave the children?

LUCY. It is useless to urge me, Auntie. I can never desert my children. I am in some sort inured to my hard fate, and shall persevere in the performance of duty to the end. I believe that in God's own good time He will set me free. I am convinced that my day of usefulness will yet come, and then my best efforts shall be put forth to alleviate the sorrows of those whom I may find have been sold as I was. I know what it is to be bound hand and foot.

AUNT. Don't talk such nonsense, child. You will never live to see the close of another year with such burdens resting upon you.

LUCY. I have looked death in the face, and fear it not. If I die, I shall be at rest, while if I go with you, an accusing conscience would embitter all my remaining days. Oh! tempt me no longer with your proffers of a home without my children. I am not to be moved from my resolution to remain with them.

AUNT. Well, Lucy, if you will not listen to my offer, I must leave you now. However, you may yet change your mind, and return to your old home. Remember that its doors will always be open to you. [GIVES LUCY MONEY.] Here are a thousand dollars.

LUCY. Many thanks for this assistance. Indeed I need it sorely. Won't you stop long enough to see Doctor Pfeifer?

AUNT. What? Stop to see that false betrayer, who by his perfidy gained you?

LUCY. Yes, stay simply to see how he will receive you.

AUNT. No. I never wish to behold his hated face again.

LUCY. Auntie, was he altogether to blame? Ought you not to have been less hasty, and waited for some confirmation of his representations?

AUNT. No doubt I should have acted more cautiously. But he came to me with such a plausible statement about his papers that I was unsuspicious of any fraudulent design on his part.

LUCY. A German baker, who lives near by and knew the Doctor in the old country, related to me the manner in which those papers came into the possession of that knave.

AUNT. How was it?

LUCY. He stole the papers from his uncle Henry, who is one of the King's officers, and they had nothing at all to do with an heirship, being merely a certificate to the effect that his uncle had received a certain sum of money from the King. He managed to deceive you as to their character by exhibiting the imposing black and red seals, and pointing to the array of signatures affixed to the documents. Your inability to read their contents enabled him the more easily to effect his design. Another circumstance I will relate: The clothes he wore when we were married were borrowed. You doubtless recollect the hair watch-chain that he showed to you and wept over, declaring that it was composed of his dead mother's hair. That, too, was a falsehood. The chain belonged to the Dutch baker referred to, and contained his mother's hair. It was returned in my presence the other day.

AUNT. [HORRIFIED.] Can this be true? Please say no more. Well, what does the false wretch possess?

LUCY. Nothing but a vile tongue and a bad temper. But I cannot help comparing his deceptive conduct in those instances with your own towards me. You robbed me of my happiness, and sold me to a life of slavery. In furthering your sordid scheme you scrupled

not to sacrifice my heart's dearest treasure, in sending my boy-lover
to the war, where he met his death upon the battle-field. You know
that you intercepted all my letters to him, which caused him to believe that I was false to my vows.

AUNT. Oh! Lucy, Lucy, your reproaches are more than I can
bear. Do not say any more. May Heaven forgive me.   [Departs.

ACT VI.

A Scene in MRS. PFEIFER's Dining Room.

CHARACTERS.—1. MISS MAMIE PFEIFER. 3. LITTLE JOHNNY PFEIFER.
          2. MISS FAIRY PFEIFER. 4. DR. PFEIFER.
                    5. MRS. LUCY PFEIFER.

The DOCTOR discovered at the dinner table. Enter the young lady,
MISS MAMIE, MISS FAIRY and JOHNNY. All sit at table and
wish their pa " Happy New Year." DOCTOR pays no attention.

LITTLE JOHNNY. Oh! papa, see what a nice turkey dinner mama
has for Johnny and papa.

DOCTOR. [BOWING.] Yes, yes, I should say it vash a shirky tinner. Only half cooked, and raw at tot.

Enter MRS. PFEIFER.

MRS. PFEIFER. [RESTING HER HAND ON THE DOCTOR'S SHOULDER.]
Now, papa, to-day is New Year's. Just as we commence to-day, so
we shall continue all through the year. Let us begin it by thanking
our Heavenly Father for all the blessings of the past, and for giving
us this beautiful new home. Let this first New Year's dinner in our
new home be one long to be remembered. Lift up your plate, Doctor. [She looks pleased. DOCTOR turns over his plate and finds an
     envelope which he looks at with searching eyes. He then
     turns to his wife, twists his nose peculiarly, and reads the
     address in a ridiculous way.

DOCTOR. " A New Yearsh vish from your ever faithful vife."
[LOOKING IN HIS WIFE'S FACE AND TWITCHING.] Hem! hem! Vat for
you vish me such shtuff as dot? Shame on yourself! Vishing tot to
a man off mine profession.

MRS. P. [PLEASED MANNER.] Open the envelope and read.

DOCTOR. [OPENS IT AND READS.] " I vish you a heppy New Year.
May it po te most bleasant vone off your life. May no dark cloud
arise to obscure its prightness."
     [Stares at MRS. P. with anger. The children and MRS. P. act
     frightened. He draws the paper over his lips in mockery,
     and insultingly flings it at MRS. P.

DOCTOR. [To MRS. P.] You old fool? Vat for you mean dark

cloud, sunshine und prightness? Koot Lort, Hefens und eart! You
crasy screechor owl. Iss tot der vay you velcome me on New Year's
tay? Vishing me such shtuff for a man off mine profession.

MRS. P. [OFFERING HIM THE BIBLE.] Come, papa, let us unite in
prayer and read a chapter in the Bible to-day.

DOCTOR. [FLINGS THE BIBLE AT HER.] Dare! You reat tot in der
hot blace. Dare you hafe blenty off gompany, You don'd hafe to in-
vite dem to come, und you see dey make it hot for you dare. [To
JOHNNY.] Dare, Shonny, get your blate, Shonny, und hafe some of
your motter's shirky-paked koose. It's notting anyhow.
[MRS. P. weeping, leaves the table.

DOCTOR. [TAKING A PIECE OF CREAM CAKE, SHOUTS TO MRS. P.]
Halloo dare! Misses, come pack. [MRS. P., WIPING HER EYES, COMES
BACK.—HE SHOWS HER THE CAKE.] Vat kint off cake you call dot?

MRS. P. It is cream cake.

DOCTOR. Vare you got cream dis dime der year? [ANGRY.] Cream
notting. [CRUMBING IT.[It's notting poot sunshine koose cravey,
put on turn ofer pie. [MRS. P. STARTS TO LEAVE THE ROOM.] Halloo!
You cot some more off dose vine vishes to-tay?
[DOCTOR throws plate on the floor and departs. MRS. P. returns.

MAMIE. How is it, mama, that we always displease our pa so?
Can you tell me? How is it that he cannot appreciate or comprehend
so simple a matter as your New Year's wishes contained in the note
you gave; and he has been through college too?

LUCY. It is very strange. I know the Germans as a class are
very intelligent and aspiring, but if he is a representative of that
kind, he does them great injustice by exhibiting his jealous and ugly
disposition. Perhaps if he had known that he was to receive a gold
watch and a set of books, he would have been more pleased.

JOHNNY. [WITH ANIMATION.] May I go in the office and tell papa
to come back and see what I has for him?

FAIRY. May I go, too, mama?

LUCY. Yes, bring him here, but talk kindly to him.
[JOHNNY and FAIRY depart.

LUCY. [TO MAMIE.] I shall give your pa the watch, and Johnny
may give him the books.

Enter FAIRY and JOHNNY with the DOCTOR.

LUCY. [GIVES DOCTOR THE WATCH.] Please excuse me, pa, for
not presenting this watch to you before. I have been busy arranging
for callers, and it slipped my mind. Let it be none the less accepta-
ble on that account.

DOCTOR. [EXAMINES THE WATCH.] It moost hafe peen off pooty
mooch importance so dot you forgot it. Vell, it's notting, anyhow.
It iss somedings I ought to hafe hat a long vile ago, for a man off
mine profession, I expected it long time ago. Done you know dot
efery man vot has a profession has vone. Dey pe common tings to
voar among shentlemen. It's notting, anyhow.

JOHNNY. [GIVES DOCTOR BOOKS.] Here, papa, is "Shakspeare's Works" and "The Arabian Nights." Johnny bought them for papa.

DOCTOR. [GIVES BACK THE BOOKS.] Vot you mean py insulting your fotter py gifing him pooks apoud "nites off shnake-shpearing?" You do as off you tink your fotter iss a know-notting, und so you gife him pooks vat he coon learn somedings py. Dot iss all your motter's notion. I vant you to know dot I hafe already got more pooks fixed in mine heat as your motter efer saw. Off you vas a loedle bicker, Shonny, you pet I voult shlam you oud toors, for insulting your fotter py gifing me pooks for a bresent. It vas all your motter's notion off putting dot in your heat. I tink it vas petter off you hat kep your money und pought me a fine pox off Havaner cigars und a pox off prandy-vine. Dot vould off make me bleased. Der whole family, in all off mine life, hafe nefer reshpec me, und shoost now you tink dot you make a man off mine profession a bresent off some pooks und a golt vatch, vat I ought to hafe hat long ago. Shouny, you petter dake dose pooks pack und gife dem to your motter, und tole her she hat petter put dem alongside off her fine New Year's vishes, und den she can hafe a bresent, too.

JOHNNY. I am not angry, pa. Why are you?

DOCTOR. You tole her for me dot I done vant any more off her Afrairican shtyle on New Year's, und none off her fine New Year's vishes eeter.   [Departs.

LUCY. [GIVES FAIRY PRESENTS.] Here is a ring and a necklace, which I hope will be accepted with more graciousness than your father's presents were.

FAIRY. [OPENS BOX.] Oh! mama. How good and kind of you to buy me just what I wanted.

LUCY. It pleases me to know that I can at least make this a happy New Year's day for my children. [GIVES JOHNNY PRESENTS.] Accept these from your mama.

JOHNNY. [GLEEFULLY.] Mama, what nice building blocks ise got, and what nice story-books. Now I can build houses, and I don't get mad because you give me books, the way pa does, do I? [KISSES HIS MOTHER.] I phwank you ten thousand times, and when I get to be a man and learn business I'll give you five hundred dollars, and if you won't cry I'll give you all my money and stay with you, and I'll never get married when I'm a man.

LUCY. I am glad you are pleased, and I want you to be a good boy.

JOHNNY. [KISSES HER.] Yes, I'll always be good to you, and don't you cry any more, will you?

MAMIE. What a sensible child he is. I'm sure he'll not be like his father when he becomes a man.

ACT VII.

Scene in a Bar-room.

CHARACTERS.—1. THE DUTCH BARKEEPER. 3. DR. PFEIFER.
2. LITTLE JOHNNY PFEIFER. 4. MISS FAIRY PFEIFER.

The Dutch Barkeeper discovered leaning on the counter in silent thought. Enter DOCTOR, leading the two children, FAIRY and JOHNNY, by the hand.

DOCTOR. [TO BARKEEPER.] Coot tay, Mishter Moshneritz.

MOHNERITZ. Coot tay, Toctor. You co off der Sherman picnic mit your shildrens? [The girl lingers in the bar-room reading a little book.

DOCTOR. Yes, sir. Poot mine grown up pick toughter. she tinks it is a shame to go mit her fatter to der Dutch picnics, as she calls dem. She von't go vere dey cife her a pick class off peer, mit wine und pologna sausage, und vere she get dreated as young latties ought to pe. [ANGRILY.] Dot is all on der gount off dot motter off hers, who sings rount all tay, breaching up der templeranclers und cold vatters all der dime. [RESTING HIS HAND ON JOHNNY'S SHOULDER.] Here, Misther Moshneritz, mine leedle poy von't pe like dot, ven he gets pick, I pet you, hay! He shmoke und trinks his glass peer und schnaps shust like a fine shentleman ought to do, und off mine profession, you know.

[JOHNNY loiters about the bar-room.

BARKEEPER. Yoost dell me vone dime how you got your Yankee vife.

DOCTOR. Yell, Mishter Moshneritz, being dat you are from mine country, I'll dell you der shtory all. But first let us hafe a glass beer.

[BARKEEPER gets a glass of beer for each. They touch glasses and the DOCTOR says: "I vish you good health."

BARKEEPER. I vish you der same and a tozen poys.

DOCTOR. Ha! ha! ha! Dot's a pooty good vish, but den I tink it's pooty pad luck. [They drink.

BARKEEPER. Go heat mit your shtory how you get your Yankee vife.

DOCTOR. You know in Sharmany, in our country dot iss near Gaetinge, der school deacher vat lives dare, und he hat two awful fine daughters. De vone married de professor off der Northeim school, und de otter vone vas bromised mit me, to be coupled togetter py law, und vat you tink, Mishter Moshneritz?

BARKEEPER. I tink dot I hear your shtory.

DOCTOR. Vell, I know dot, but dat girl Babbit, I fool mit her for long six year. Vell, der tay vas setted ven ve should be coupled togetter py der law off mine country. Vell, frient Moshneritz, done you tink dot I talk der English awful foorst shtreight?

BARKEEPER. Vell, Toctor, vere iss your shtory? You ditn't get any vider don vere you vas coupled togetter py law.

DOCTOR. Oh, vell, I forgot mineself. I vas tinking off mine profession. Ve nefer vas coupled togetter.

BARKEEPER. Vell, you shtop mit your shtory. You ditn't finish it all.

DOCTOR. Vell, Mishter Moshneritz, yoost gife me anotter glass beer to vet mine troat, und den I goed on mit mine shtory vere ve shtop. [EACH DRINKS ANOTHER GLASS OF BEER.] Vell, in der firsht dime, der vas sooch an goot for notting nopoty. He goed und tole Babbit's father dot I trink so mooch beer, und blav on der carts mit mine money, vich you know I don't do. I don't blay on der carts. I done tink dot iss mooch for an ordinary shentleman und off mine profession to trink efery tay a leedle someding, like twenty-fife glass beer, und vonce in a vile a glass brandy-vine. I done tink dot iss pooty mooch. Yoost tink off dot goot-for-notting nopoty dolling sooch shtuff apoud a man off mine profession. Vell, don'd I tole you yoost now dot on der next Sunday, ven I vent to see mine leedle Babbit vat you tink I got?

BARKEEPER. I tink I hear your shtory.

DOCTOR. Ven I got dare und I rap on der toor, her fotter coom off der toor und shpeaked to me: "Vat you vant here? You tink you blay beer und trink carts all der night troo, und don you show your face on mine toor, und vant to see mine girl Babbit?" Den he tole me: " Make mit yourself off, und nefer coom here again. You dock you? You notting you!" Den he tole me hiss Babbit vas going to marry a rich man der next veek, und don't you tink I done pooty goot ven I coom off America?

BARKEEPER. Vat shall I tink? I tink I vait for your shtory.

DOCTOR. Vell, as you he from mine blace, dot iss Hanover, I'll tole you how I make it mit her, dat iss Babbit. In der firsht blace, I tink I like her pooty much goot, und ven I tinks off her I feel somedings in mine shtomach vat keeps saying, " Shoomp up, shoomp up in mine troat," so pick as a great pick glass beer, und I lofe to set on a chair mit py her site, und delle her all how I shtudy off der school, und I learn mine bick Toctor profession.

BARKEEPER. Vell, Doctor, pe you treaming? Vat iss your profession to do mit der shtory apoud how you got Yankee vife? Dot is der question pefore dis saloon shoost now.

DOCTOR. Vait vonce, mine frient, until I tole you apoud mine profession, und den I'll tole you dat it got eferyting to do mit her—mine profession has. I dells you if a man keeps himself streight, und has got a bick profession like I got a profession, I tell you he coon coom vide nit himself ofer diss country.

BARKEEPER. Vell, off you don'd vant to dell apoud your Yankee vife firsht, den dell me firsht apoud your profession.

DOCTOR. Vell, I tink I dell you now vat I vas going to tole you— vat you tink?

BARKEEPER. Vell, you ask me all der dime [LAUGHING] vat I tink. I dell you I vait a long dime for your shtory. I vant to hear it firsht, den I vill dell you petter vat I tink. '

DOCTOR. Vell, shoost tink. I tought me und I treamed dot I like Babbit pooty vell, und den I feel dot great pick beer mit der glass cooming up in mine troat, saying, " You lofe Babbit or you lofe me?" Dot you know vas yoost pefore Babbit's fotter gave me a bick shmell von der toes off his boots ride on mine chin. [POINTS TO HIS CHIN.] I tink you see dot mark on mine chin. Dot vas der blace vere der admittance vas off his boot. I tink dot mark last yet for sometime. Babbit's fotter done py me shoost like he vould do py hiss pick plack hoont called Carlo, und he says, " Make oud mit yourself." I dell you I felt pooty shmall for a man off mine profession ven he kicked me oud.

BARKEEPER. Hem! hem! Vas dot Lucy on der count? Vas dot on der count off your Yankee vife? You don't tell me. Vas dot Lucy on der count you hat dot drouble from her fotter?

DOCTOR. [HURRIEDLY.] No, no! Dot vas yet in Sharmany. Dot vas Babbit, der school teacher's girl. Vone night pefore I go off der ped, dot vas pefore I go off shleep, you know.

BARKEEPER. Vat you tink I know?

DOCTOR. Oh! you put me oud, done you know? Vell, I ask mine heart vonce in dis vay, vonce, twice, three times, you tell me pefore der morning cooms, und answer me dis question, " Do I lofe Babbit or don't I lofe Babbit enough to make her mine vife py law?" Und vat you tink? Mine heart pefore der next morning answered me No. Und den vat you tink? I say to mineself, [WITH DISGUST] "P ooh! pooh!" Den vat you tink? I tought noddings off her any more.

BARKEEPER. [SMILINGLY.] Vell, yell. I don't vonder me any dot you don lofe her any after Lucy's fotter trowed you oud off der house mit a shmell off his boot, und vat goot dit your profession do you den?

DOCTOR. Done I tole you? I neffer married her. I got Lucy to pe mine vife, und mittout shmelling off a Yankee boot eeter off her fotter's, pecause Lucy ditn't hafe any fotter, pecause he vent tead pefore she vas too young to pe mine vife.

BARKEEPER. [GRINS.] I tink so mineself. How dit you make it so dot you got your Yankee vife?

DOCTOR. Shenk me oud some beer, und den I tole you how I hoombuged in dis country for a man off mine profession.

BARKEEPER. [GIVES HIM BEER.] Take dis beer now mit mine best vishes dot you nefer hafe to shmell anotter boot off der school teachers mit oud off der house.

DOCTOR. Vell, mine frient Moshneritz, I'll tole you first apoud mine profession und how I got him. In der first blace, mine frient, mine fotter vas a poor man, und his profession vas a barber. Now, you know mit his barber profession he didn't get not mooch money,

und I vas der only son, und remember it vas not mine fodder vat sent
me off der school. It vas mine uncle Heinrich who sented me off der
bick academy. In dot academy der poys from efery kingdom vear a
tifferent color of clothes. Shoost tink, von dime, how fine I looked,
und how der scholars looked off me ven dey see me coom in mit mine
brass buttons und mine golt glasses vat I vear on mine heat pefore
mine eyes. Oh! Moshneritz, yoost tink how nice I looked, und I
valked so shtreight mit mine new clothes on; but dot maked no tifference you know, pecause I carry von shoulder higher dan der otter
von. I nefer looked to der left otter to der right to see who looked
off me, boot anyhow I knew dat dey all looked off me, und der vis-
pered von to der otter: "Dare is der Doctor Pfeifer, mit his golt
glasses unt mit his valking shtick mit a golt heat shtanding on him."
I knew dot dey all honored me, shoost pecause I tried to act so
schmart, und didn't talk mooch, und I didn't look on der otter scholars. I remember dot dey always laughed offer mine fine heat off
hair, und den I feel proud.

BARKEEPER. [LAUGHING.] Vell, vell, Toctor, vere is your hair
now gone? I see you ain't got mooch left.

DOCTOR. Vell, frient Moshneritz, ven I vos young yet, und only
twenty-five, und done you say notting to anypoty. Now I pesh
pooty mooch fifty-fife; but done you say notting, for I tell mine Yankee vife all der dime dot I pesh thirty-three. Now, I tole you dot von
dime ven I vas twenty-fife, I vas sick mit der fefer, und mine hair in
shoost von night all flew out quick—ff't—ff't—und den it vas all ofer.

BARKEEPER. Vell, Toctor, you hat pooty pat luck already. You
ought to hafe good luck vonc dime for a change.

DOCTOR. Goot luck? You petter bet, I got goot luck. I go mit
mine shildrens to-tay off der Sherman picnics. [SHOWS CANE.] You
see dot valking shtick dare, mit der golt heat on him? I vas going to
tole you vonce pefore apoud der hishtory off dot shtick. You know,
von tay, ven der professor off der examinations asks der shtudents
somedings in questions apoud vat he tinks dey know und dey done
know. Und von tay ven he cooms in und ve ditn't reshpect him, und
den ve all trembled und ve hat to write down vat questions he asked
us shtudents. Der first question vas, "How many tays hafe ve got in
der year, und in vat year is dis dot ve now got?" Some off der shtudents answered notting. He asked vone und he asked dem all, und
some didn't know, untl some shook der heats und said, "I done know."
Und I den pegan to shtreighten mineself up, ven he coom to me und
he said, "Vell, Heinrich Pfeifer, coon you dell me how many tays dot
ve got in der year?" Den I shtreightened mineself up und hollered
und shpoke lout: "Ve gat a leedle ofer two tousant und fife hundert."
Den der whole school house, mit der brofessors und scholars, commenced to laugh yoost awful to tink dot I was so shmart. Den der
brofessor took oud his bick book und wrote down someding in mine
honor, und den gafe me dis valking-shtick und tole me, "You alvays
keep dot, und not part mit him."

BARKEEPER. Vell, Toctor, are you treaming? I vaited for your shtory, how you got your Yankee vife. I vould like to hear it, dot is off you hafe got troo mit your profession. I pet you off you voult travel mit sooch a theatre or a circus, und you voult dell your shtory der vey dot you tole me shoost now, I pet you vould make more money den you do mit your Toctor profession; dot is off you voult tole your shtory der vey dot you tole me in dis saloon. You make money I pet you. You valk mit vone shoulder higher den der otter, shoost like von off dose theatre fellers, und you shwing rount der same vey mit your valking shtick.

DOCTOR. Vell, Moshneritz, now I'll tole you yoost how I done ven I got Lucy. In der first blace, der brofessor off der school in Goetinge, he gafe me a groat long paper mit plack und red zeals mit der names off der gounselmens on dem.

BARKEEPER. Vat for you got tem bapers?

DOCTOR. Dose papers I got vas for der attmittance to go pack und shtay ofer tree years again pecause I ditn't pass mit der examination. All der otter scholars vat vent ven I dit got dere certificates to shtay home. Der reason vy I ditn't got mine ven dey dit vas pecause I vas so far aheat off tem dot I couldn't answer von question dot der brofessor asked me, und der otters answered efery ting. Now py dot you see I hat to go pack off school und shtay tree years longer, und pegin vere I dit on der first dime und vere der otters left off. I dell you dem vas hart shtudy tays, und I hat to commence ofer to learn mine profession, und der otters hat gone home to practice deirs alreaty. I dell you ven I got troo I vas pooty mooch so shmart as der otters vas. So mine uncle tole me it is pettor off I go off America, und he voult gife me money off I voult leafe der country, for I coult do petter in America mit mine profession, as I coot in sooch a shmall country as Europe. He tole me dot I coot come vider und shtant higher in a shtrange country as I voult in Sharmfany.

BARKEEPER. I tink you done pooty goot to get as vide as you hafe in der New York.

DOCTOR. You know I hafe got a certificate from dot academy, und dot dey gafe me so as to make me remember dot I vas von dime off college.

BARKEEPER. [IMPATIENTLY.] Vere is your Yankee vife all off dis time dot you learn your profession?

DOCTOR. Oh! She is to home to-day, und vashes und takes care off her house vork mit her papy.

BARKEEPER. You don'd forshtand me, Toctor. I meant vere vas your Yankee vife ven you vas learning your profession?

DOCTOR. Vell, off you don'd know I'll tole you vere she vas. She vas in America und I vas in Sharmany mit off der school—voult you tink dot?

BARKEEPER. [LAUGHING.] Vell, Toctor, you hafe a pooty awful long shtory, und I don'd know yet how you got your Yankee vife. I hafe drinked so many glass beer mit you und shtill I know not how you coom by your vife. Vat you tink I care apoud how you done mit your Babbit in Sharmany? It's your Yankee vife dot I vant to know from.

DOCTOR. Done I tole you, friend Moshneritz, dot von timo, ven I vent to see mine uncle Heinrich, mit his fino tings on his shoulders, und he vent oud off der door, I saw some great pick papers hang on' der writing table, mit der names off dose pick gounselmen's names on dem, und der right corner hat a pick red seal, und der left corner hat a pick plack seal, you know. I tought dot I voult shtole dem und it make notting oud mit mine uncle Heinrich, for he hat his pay alreaty, und dot baper vas his reception telling dot he hat got his money alreaty und it make him notting oud. You pet it mate efery ting oud mit me. Vell, I tole you, frient Moshneritz, dot I heard von dime dot der Americans liked hoonbug. Vell, shoost tink, ven I ' coom off dis country, I vas valking oud von morning mit der shtreet up und town, making folks beliefe mit mine medicine box dot I vas going to visit some batients, und vat you tink? I saw a great pick plack horse mit on der man's pack, on a saddle, und der man vent, " Hoory up! hoory up!" und vat you tink who dot vas?

BARKEEPER. Vat shoult I tink? I tink dat I hear your shtory. I don'd know.

DOCTOR. Vell, done I tole you, dot vas Mishter Lillapritge, Lucy's unclo. Vell, you know he vas sooch a rich man, und Lucy lived mit him und her aunt, und he vanted a Toctor pooty quick for his vife vat vas awful sick. He saw mit me on der shtreet, mit mine golt shpectacles on mine heat pefore mine eyes, und he saw me shwing along mit mine valking shtick mit der golt heat shtand on him, und he hollered, " Halloo dare! Mishter, oxcoose me. Coult you tolt me vere I fint der Toctor?" I tolt him dot I pesh der Toctor Pfeifer by profession, und not long oud from Sharmany. Den he hollered, " All right, mine shentleman. Coom mit me off mine house, und see mine laty," unt I vent mit him to see her. Vell, she got vell pooty quick, und ven she vas so dot sho sot up mit on her chair, und in her great pick fine room, den she asked me von tay, " Toctor, you moost coom von dime pooty quick und soe me." Und I tole you, I vent pooty quick, und den I tole her all apoud mine profession, und how I got him. Von dime I hert dat der Yankees nefer beliefe anyting mitout dey moost see der papers to prove tings, und ven I tole her apoud my heirship von tay, I tole her dot I voult show her der papers. Den sho invited me von dime to coom und get acquainted mit Lucy, und den I vent; und der second dime I prought mit me der papers und showed dem to her aunt, und it made notting oud if her aunt coultn't reat der Sharman so long as dey was papers, und dot vos der vey I hoombuged. Der aunt und me made it all oud how ve shoult fix it to get married, und Lucy hat to mind und marry me. Der first dime dot I saw Lucy mine heart vent once more, " Shoomp up, shoomp up!" und

I tole you, I felt so happy to tink dot I coult make oud mine profession I coult get Lucy. Vell, und ven I shpeaked mit Lucy, she tole me, "No, sir, I not marry a Sharman, und I not like you, und I nefer marry an ugly Sharman like you." Den she criet unt wrung her hants unt sait, "I nefer coon marry you, ole Dutchman." Ven she sait dot I mate beliefe dot I not undershtand. Und remember, her aunt mate beliefe to Lucy dot I vas coming der next tay for tea, und den ve go off a fine tress party. Und in der blace off der tress party der minister vas engaged, und it vas too late for Lucy to shpeak, und she vas mate to do as she vas tole py her aunt, und vat you tink? Inshted off der tress party ve vas coupled togetter py law.

BARKEEPER. Is dot der vey you hoombuged? I tink you done it pooty quick. Where is all your heirship to-tay?

DOCTOR. Vell, you know, I ditn't get any money. It vas hoombug, und she hat lots off money dot she got after ve vere married a year, den ve got us a nice house, und ve inwested in a farm off coal, und she pought me five tousant tollars vorth off inshtruments und pooks for mine office, unt I hat it in mine house, und you pet I make her vork und do as I tole her.

BARKEEPER. How vos dat dot she is sooch a goot voman, und forshpends so mooch money on her shildrens?

DOCTOR. You know efery morning und efery tay, I tole her und maked her beliefe dot she has been doing somedling wrong, und for instance, like shpeaking mit anotter man, und py dot she gets so sheared dot she is afrait to do somedings wrong, und I always hafe a goot voman. I tole her shtoof before I know anyting apoud it.

BARKEEPER. Vell, Toctor, I tink you hafe coom oud pooty goot mit your hoombug.

DOCTOR. [TURNS TO JOHNNY.] Here is mine leedle poy, und you pet I make him a nice shentleman, shoost sooch a vone as der Yankees like. I make him so dot he coon hoombug shoost like his fotter.

MOSHNERITZ. Say, leedle poy, vat is your name, sir?

JOHNNY P. Johnny Pfeifer.

DOCTOR. [SHAKING THE BOY'S ARM.] Dot ish not Yoney. It ish Shonny Pfeifer. You must not talk so Yankee shtyle, like your motter. Now say Yonny.

JOHNNY P. Yonny Pfeifer.

DOCTOR. [TO BARKEEPER.] Don'd you tink he pe a shmart poy? He coon shbell shust like nottings at all, I tell you. I vill hafe him shbell vone dime for you, den you draw for him oud off him a vone pick glass peer. [TO JOHNNY.] Now I vant you to shbell vone dime for us. Now, Shonny, Mishter Moshneritz, mine frient, vants you to shbell—now—Shonny—shbell "dock," der name off your Carlo dot you hitch after your hant-shleigh.

JOHNNY. [SPELLS.] D-o-g, dog. [The barkeeper looks pleased.

DOCTOR. [SHAKING JOHNNY'S ARM.] I didn't dell you to shbell dough. Vat ish der matter? It's petter you dry vonce more. I meant you shbell tock, der name off your Carlo. Remember vat I tole you.   •

JOHNNY. Talk? T-a-l-k, talk.

DOCTOR. [MUCH PLEASED.] Vell, Shonny, you posh right. You make somedimes a shmart mans, hay?

MOSHNERITZ. [GRINNING.] Ho pesh a nice poy, yes.

DOCTOR. Now, Mishter Moshneritz, you ket a pick class peer for der poy. [BARKEEPER GIVES BEER TO DOCTOR, WHO OFFERS IT TO JOHNNY.] Dare, Shonny, take dot.

JOHNNY. [CRYING.] Oh! papa, I don't like it. Mama said I must not drink any.   ‎

DOCTOR. Now, Shonny, you must trink dot peer, und pe a man, und not hear to your motter mit her demperance all der dime, und cold vater. I am your fatter und a Toctor is mine profession. I tink you petter mlud me, inshtead of hearing dot sing-song koruss off your motter—all der dime templeranclers.

JOHNNY. I don't care. I don't want any. I'll mind my mama.

BARKEEPER. [RESTING HIS HAND ON THE BOY'S HEAD.] You pe right. Dot is right, mine poy. Always mint your motter.

DOCTOR. [DRINKING THE BEER QUICKLY.] Now, Mishter, gife me a glass off schnapps. [BARKEEPER GIVES HIM WHISKY.—SHOUTS TO FAIRY.] Coom, Fairy, have someting.

FAIRY. I just had some.   [Looks on the book.

DOCTOR. [GIVES THE GLASS TO JOHNNY.] Now, Shonny, you take diss und trink it.   [JOHNNY puts it untouched on the counter.

BARKEEPER. Dot is too strong for der poy, Toctor. He is right to not drink it.

DOCTOR. Vat for you site mit mine vife? You pen shpeaking mit her? Dot's a pooty vay to talk to a man off mine profession.

BARKEEPER. Vell, Toctor, I tink your fife is pooty mooch right. You petter keep your money to puy preat mit for your shildrens, so dot your fife not vork herself to death mit all kints off vork. Dat looks mooch petter for you.

DOCTOR. Vat—vat for you keep dis saloon?   ‎

BARKEEPER. I keep dis saloon for all dose beoples vat can behafe demsolf teasant. I ditn't ask you to coom in here. [POINTS TO THE DOOR.] You valk mit yourself right shtreight oud off der tor.

DOCTOR. Poot you take mine money.

BARKEEPER. Yes, sir. Und you dake mine peer und schnapps. I dell you again, make mit your toughter, your poy und your shildrens oud off here.

DOCTOR. [ASHAMED.—TO HIS CHILDREN.] Coom't on. Halloo dare! Ve go off der Sharman picnics nit ourself.

[DOCTOR takes children's hands and staggers out.

ACT VIII.

SCENE—DOCTOR at Dutch Picnic.

CHARACTERS.—1. DOCTOR PFEIFER.   3. JOHNNY.
               2. FAIRY.   4. HANS, a waiter.
                   5. People at another picnic table.

The DOCTOR is discovered at the picnic table. The girl sits at his right and the girl at his left. HANS is waiting on the people at the other table.

DOCTOR. [SHOUTS TO HANS.] Coom't on! Halloo! Pring me und mine shildrens somedings to drink.

JOHNNY. [WHISPERS TO FAIRY.] What shall we do? Pa is now drunk and calls for something more.

FAIRY. Go quick. Tell the waiter not to give him any more beer..

JOHNNY. Oh! no. I dare not. He will punish us. What will mama do to-night?

Enter waiter with a plate of bolognas, three glasses of beer and a plate of fried cakes, which he puts down. DOCTOR drinks his beer and the children slyly pour their's on the ground, pretending, when their father turns to them, that they have drank it.

DOCTOR. [TO CHILDREN.] You pe right. You pe shmart to-tay to trink your peer.

[Looks around and then in an awkward manner hands each of the children a piece of bologna, saying:

DOCTOR. Eat dat quick. I hafe to pay ten cents to get admittances off der picnic. You vill not get for a good vile sooch a chance again. [POINTS TO THE PLATES.] Dare, stick dem sausages und dem cakes in your pockets. Quick, pefore folks see you.

[The children both fill their coat pockets with sausage and fried cakes, allowing the ends to project from each pocket. The DOCTOR, looking first for a chance, fills his silk hat with fried cakes, leaving only a few on each plate.

DOCTOR. [TO HANS.—PUTS ON HIS HAT.] Halloo dare! Pring me on tree glass prandy-vine. [HANS DEPARTS.—TO CHILDREN.] Come, come. Quick take dem last sausages und cakes, und shtick dem in.

JOHNNY AND FAIRY. [TOGETHER.] I can't. I haven't any more room. [The DOCTOR slyly takes the last sausages and forces them up into his hat, which he holds with one hand on his head, meanwhile looking around. The crown bursts and the sausages and cakes fall out on each side of him. He acts as if wondering where they come from. Still they fall more than ever. At that moment HANS enters with wine which puts he down at DOCTOR's side. The latter looks surprised at seeing HANS.

DOCTOR. [LOOKS AROUND.] Oh! oxcoose me. I go to shtoop mineself up, und knocked der blates off der tables.

[The crowd at the picnic laugh heartily.

HANS. [LOOKS AT DOCTOR.] Oh! It's too bat. Tings like dot often happens. I seen it all.

DOCTOR. [POINTING TO THE FALLEN SAUSAGES.] Coom, shiltren, pick dem up und put dem pack on der blates.

[The waiter joins the crowd in laughing at the DOCTOR. The children leave their pockets filled as they are. DOCTOR drinks the three glasses of liquor. Crowd all laugh.

DOCTOR. Oh! shiltrens, don't I vish dat I hat all off dose shblendit sausages und cakes. Oh! darn it. [SHOUTS TO CROWD.] Dot vas all on der gound off dot fife off mine. She upsetted eferyting und mine profession. She upsetted me und eferyting else. [CROWD LAUGH.—CHILDREN ASHAMED.—TO CHILDREN.] Com't on. Halloo, shiltren. Halloo. Ve go home.

[DOCTOR fixes his hat tighter on his head. The crown of the hat hangs by a couple of threads only. DOCTOR, taking the two children by the hand, starts to leave the picnic. After going a few steps, a piece of bologna falls out of the girl's pocket. All stop. The girl picks it up and replaces it in her pocket. The crowd laugh and shout. After going a few steps further, the sausages again fall. They continue walking and looking back at the sausages. DOCTOR staggers against the girl, causing her to fall.

ACT IX.

SCENE I.—LUCY'S Kitchen.

CHARACTERS—1. LUCY.   4. DOCTOR.
2. FAIRY.   5. AUNTIE FLAGAN.
3. JOHNNY.

LUCY discovered in the kitchen, holding her infant with one arm, and washing with her disengaged hand.

Enter FAIRY and JOHNNY. LUCY looks pleased.

CHILDREN. [IN CHORUS.] Oh! mama, mama. Pa is drunk. He is so mad because we wouldn't drink beer. He wants to kill us all.

[LUCY is frightened.

JOHNNY. Hurry up.

FAIRY. Let us run away.

LUCY. God bless you, dear children.

Enter DOCTOR, staggering to his wife.

DOCTOR. [CATCHES LUCY BY THE THROAT.] Here is hell for you.
[DOCTOR falls sprawling on the floor, helpless. The children
and LUCY with her infant run away screaming.

SCENE II.—JOHNNY, FAIRY and LUCY with her infant are crossing a
stream of water on planks. It is moonlight, and the
rocks and banks are separated by streamlets. LUCY,
when almost across the stream, holds out her hand for
JOHNNY, and then peers through the rocks.

LUCY. Oh! children, come quick. Let's hurry before pa comes
after us. [All wade through safely to the other side. As they reach
the bank all kneel in silent prayer.

Enter AUNTIE FLAGAN from behind some rocks, drawing a hand-cart
containing two empty milk pails.

AUNTIE FLAGAN. [INTERRUPTING THE PRAYING FAMILY.] Oh! en
for th' luv uv Saint Pathric! En is it you agin? Ah! en the Laird
save us. [THE FAMILY WEEP.] Dair swaitings, [IN ONE BREATH] en
can yer tell me what brought yez over here this night? Uv coorse
it's that divil uv a mon agin. En nivir moind—the divil 'ill be shakin'
him over purgatory some day. En me dair crathurs, nivir moind.
[WIPES HER EYES WITH APRON.—IN WEEPING VOICE.] En it's me that
saves ye this time.

[AUNTIE FLAGAN puts the little girl in the cart, and gives her
the infant to hold. LUCY leads the little boy. AUNTIE
FLAGAN draws the cart, exclaiming: " Come, ye dair
little swaiting, I'll take yez home." All depart.

ACT X.

SCENE—DOCTOR rising from his stupor.

CHARACTER.—THE DOCTOR.

The DOCTOR discovered moving on the floor where he fell in the
kitchen. He gets up slowly, rubbing his eyes and looks
around. He scratches his head, yawns and straightens
himself. He then jumps up and down, shouting, " Lucy."
Opens a door and peers into a room; then shuts the door
with a slam; opens another door and does same thing.

DOCTOR. [SHOUTS.] Mrs. Pfeifer! Lucy, Lucy! Lucy Pfeifer!
Halloo dare! [OPENS A DOOR.] Vere in der teills you shtick yourself?
Shonny! Shonny! Shonny, mine son! [SHAKING HIS HEAD.] I shoost
like to know vere tem tefils nations putted temselves to.

[He opens a door again and gets a bonnet; then slamming the
door, he grunts with rage, and throws the bonnet in the
wash-boiler, pounding it down with a stick, saying:

"Oh! off dot vas only your prains, Lucy Pfeifer, inshtead off your bonnet."

Grunting, the DOCTOR takes a table-cloth, dishes and
other things and throws them all in the boiler. He then
stands the baby cab on the stove, saying:

"Dare, I purn der tefils oud off you."

ACT XI.

SCENE I.—MRS. LUCY PFEIFER'S Parlor.

CHARACTERS.—1. LUCY.   4. JOHNNY.
        2. MAMIE.   5. THE DOCTOR.
        3. FAIRY.

MAMIE is discovered playing on the piano. LUCY is sewing. FAIRY
crocheting. Enter JOHNNY.

JOHNNY. Where has pa been?

LUCY. I don't know, Johnny.

Enter DOCTOR. FAIRY and JOHNNY remain standing. MAMIE stops
playing.

DOCTOR. Halloo dare, shiltren und Lucy. I got somedings vat I
vant to tole you. [TO LUCY AND MAMIE.] Set mit yourselfs shtill on
der chair. [TO JOHNNY AND FAIRY.] Make mit yourselfs oud, und
don'd you dare to come mit your feet pefore mine heat until I tole
you. [FAIRY AND JOHNNY DEPART.—TO LUCY AND MAMIE.] I vant to
tole you somedings vat is off a great importance und off a great af-
fluence. It is somedings dot shoost transmitted shoost now, a leedle
vile ago, dis dime.

LUCY. [WITH SURPRISE.] You don't say that something terrible
transpired to-day, do you?

DOCTOR. Oh, yas, yas. Der transmittance shoost now happened
in Fritz Grootenheimer's saloon.

LUCY. What can it be? Have you been in the saloon?

DOCTOR. Dot makes nodding oud. Vait until I tole you, und
don'd any off you shpeak until you see der towel shake.

LUCY. I wonder if any one has been killed.

DOCTOR. No, no. [TO MAMIE.] Look mit your fotter shtreight
mit in his face, und I vant you to undershtand vat I shpeak mit you.
Vat you tink?

MAMIE. Tell me, first, papa, then I shall say what I think.

DOCTOR. Is dot der vay you shpeak to your fotter ven he tole
you somedings? Do you mean to say do you nefer tink off it after-
wards? Vait vonce, von dime. I show you how to tink somedings
to-morrow.

MAMIE. You misunderstand me. I shall think of it.

DOCTOR. Halloo, Mamie. Now hark to vat I tole you. I vant you to be harking to efery vord vat I tole you.

Dono you know der year after dis, ven I shpeaked mit you, und I tole you apoud der pick rich Count Martrit, vat lifes in Hanover, in a pick cashteel, shoost like der King?

MAMIE. Yes, I remember you told me about Count Martrit who lives in a castle.

DOCTOR. Vell, der fetter off der Count owns great pick cashteels in all der cities nearly in efery kingdom all ofer Europe, und he owns sooch great pick vide farms, vere der vood grows dot ve use to keep der fire warm mit. Und shoost tink vonce ven you coon go off Sharmany und see dem cashteels.

MAMIE. It would be grand; but what has the Count to do with me?

DOCTOR Can't you vait until I tole you, und den you'll see dot he has eferyting mit you to do.

MAMIE. Very well. I'm prepared to hear your story.

DOCTOR. Oh, mine grashus. See. Der Afrairicans dey nefer coon vait mit der mout shtill ven deir fotters vants to shpeak mit dem. Dey ought to learn vat der Shermans tole deir shiltrens. Dey dell dem dot dey shoult nefer shpeak until der towel shakes, und den it gifes dem to undershtand dot it iss deir turn to shpeak somedings.

LUCY. Why don't you proceed with your story, Doctor? Mamie is listening.

DOCTOR. Dare it is. Vat dit I tole you? Der Afrairicans mit deir Afrairican shtyle, upsetted eferyting. Vat dit I shoost tole you, Lucy Pfeifer? Dit you see der towel shake? You upsetted me completely efery dime, so dot I nefer coon tole dot vat I hafe reaty on mine tongue to tole you. Vat for you always upset me? Der Afrairican voman always upset deir hushbants any vay.

LUCY. Proceed. We are all listening.

DOCTOR. Remember und not shpeak somedings until you see der towel shake, den you coon undershtand dot you hafe der admittance to shpeak.

LUCY. Proceed.

DOCTOR. Hold on. To-morrow I pring in dis house pefore your eyes der Honorable Sir Count Martrit, und I shoost coom from der saloon vere I coom from shpeaking mit him und trinking ein glass beer. He vas sooch a fine Sherman, und from Hanover, mine country; und shoost tink vonce, he shtudied apoud der medicines, und he vill make a pick Toctor py profession, und he vears a heafy golt vatch mit a heafy golt chain; und his vatch is shoost like efery man's dot has a profession und vears one; und vat you tink? He valks mit der shtreet mit a valking shtick mit in his hant, und he has sooch pooty fine hair, shoost like mine, und he looks oud off his eyes shoost der same vay dot I do, und in his face he looks somedings like me. Don'd you forget now, Mamie, vat I tole you. He vas der only vone son,

und his motter ha*, vent tead ven he vas tree years olt alroaty. Now,
remember vat I tole you, Mamie. To-morrow, ven I pring him here
to dis house, und I set him down to tole you somedings, you moost
hafe some reshspect for him, und not show off as ven you tink he is a
man mitout a profession, for von you see his pick golt vatch you can
see dot ho has a profession.

MAMIE. Certainly, papa. I shall entertain him.

DOCTOR. Dot is all right. Now, I am going to tole you vat der
Count Martrit tole me in Fritz Grootenhelmer's saloon. He tole me
dot von his motter vas tead he used to run efery dime dot der pick
gates vas open in der grafeyard, und he used to go und shtand ofer
his tead motter's grafe, und hold fast on der pick ornaments mit his
hants und pray. Und dose pick ornaments und monuments vat
shtand ofer der blaco vere his motter is puried, each vone costed ofer
tree tousant tollars, und der names off der pick gounselmens shtand
on dem.

MAMIE. Why are the councilmen's names engraved on the monuments?

DOCTOR. Der monuments are put ofer his motter's grafe so as to
make der Count und otter beoples remember dot his motter vas tead
von dime. Shoost tink vonce how nice it is ven you can see dem.

MAMIE. That is all very well, but how does it concern me?

DOCTOR. Voll, shoost shtop a leedle, und den I vill tole you pooty
quick. You vill see to-morrow dot ven dot fine Count comes mit his
pick Toctor profession, he vill shpeak eeter French, Sherman or English mit you. I vant you to remember dot you moost say yes to eferyting dot he asks you.

MAMIE. Why shall I say yes to everything he asks me?

DOCTOR. You undershtand, done you, your fotter is a pooty ole
man, und off you vill make yourself undershtand, und shoost tink
dot you hafe got a fotter vat vould like to travel mit himself all ofer
off Hanover, und go mit himself to Paris, und see all off der vine cities vat shtand dare, und ven you tink pooty mooch off your ole fotter, you vill do dot mooch as to say yes to der Count Martrit. Vat
you tink?

MAMIE. What do you mean, papa? I have no money as yet in my
possession to afford your seeing the old country once more.

DOCTOR. Oh! no, no, no. You be shoost like all off der Afrairicans know nottings, und your motter, vat po always toleing dot vat
dev done know. Done I tole you dot I fetch der young Count Martrit mit his pick Toctor profession to shpeak mit you und tole you
somedings, und I hope dot you show yourself off as a young lady
shoult mit your fine laukguage, und done you show off as ven you
vas nefer off der semilinary or school, und as ven you done know
how to shpell.

MAMIE. Certainly, papa, I shall treat him with respect, but it is
hardly necessary to tell him that I know how to spell.

DOCTOR. You done know notting ven I tole you so often, und shtill you done undershtand me. Alvays ven your Afrairican motter mit her society und shtyle tole you somedings, it is alvays, " Oh, yes, yes, mama." But ven I shpeak mit you, it is shoost like nottings at all.

MAMIE. What shall I do and say? I have not disobeyed you. Explain, please.

DOCTOR. How mooch plainer shall I tole you? I talk der English shoost so plain as anypoty, und shoost like nottings at all. Done you undershtand dot I got by dis dime der algebra fixt in mine heat shoost so goot as you und your motter. I tole you so often already dot ven a man has der algebra fixt in his heat so goot as I got it, he coon shpeak shoost sooch fine lankguage as I can.

MAMIE. Yes, you talk very well, considering your advantages in this country.

DOCTOR. For example, when I coom in der house somedimes, und I fint you und your motter talking apoud der Longfellow's poems, und der Shnakeshpearing, und Botany, vot tole you all apoud how der shtars are fixt vat hang ofer your heat, you alvays undershtand her und you say yes. Why done you nefer undershtand me ven I talk English plainer as your motter, for I can nefer undershtand her?

MAMIE. I always understand you after you have explained your meaning.

DOCTOR. Vat for you vent off der school to learn to shpell, ven you done undershtand der English lankguage like vat I talk? I hope you vill say yes ven der Count comes.

MAMIE. I understand you perfectly, and when your friend comes I shall be entertaining. You don't mean that I shall kiss a stranger or embrace him, I hope.

DOCTOR. Yes. If der Count shpeaks mit you for a kiss to-morrow, you gife him von—or two or tree, for dot matter.

MAMIE. What do you mean? How absurd.

DOCTOR. I mean dot you shall not show off der vey your motter dit ven vo vas pooty mooch reaty to pe coupled togetter py law.

MAMIE. What did she do when you ventured to kiss her the first time?

DOCTOR. She acted like ven she vas crasy, und she gafe me a bick schare, so dot I vas afrait to kiss her again. Ven der Count makes lofe to you, you moost not shoomp up from your shair like your motter done, und run like crasy as off you pe a shicken mitout your heat on. You remember dot ven he asks you to pe his vife, you moost act pleased, und not do as your motter done, to run like crasy, or else he vill hafe a pad opinion off you.

MAMIE. I perceive. You mean marriage, do you?

DOCTOR. Yes. Der Count is rich, und you moost marry him.

MAMIE. Impossible. I cannot marry him.

DOCTOR. I pet you vill. I'll pring him here to-morrow, after der
train gets in. He has got so mooch money, und I shpeaked mit him
to-tay. You moost mind your fotter, und none off your Afrairican
foolishness mit lofe like your motter. Der Count tole me dot he
vanted an Afrairican vife, und she moost know how to blay und sing
off der piano, und she moost know how to talk French, English und
der Sherman lankguages. Und he tole me dot she moost gratuate alreaty from der sumarary.

MAMIE. Why must I possess all of these accomplishments?

DOCTOR. I done know. It is pecause he is a man vat has a profession like me. After der Count tole me all off dot, I tole him dot I
hat a fine toughter vat vas apoud sixteen years old, und I tole him
you coult blay mit der piano, und dot you coult sing shoost like a
pluejay.

MAMIE. Why did you tell him that?

DOCTOR. I tole him all apoud you pecause he is a man vat·has a
profession, und den he tole me off all off dis pe for ferteldy, vich is a
Sherman Latin vord, und means off English true.

MAMIE. I understand.

DOCTOR. Und now you hold on vat I tole you. To-morrow,
ven der Count Martrit asks you to pe coupled togetter py law, you
moost act pleased, und say yes, und you pe shtill like a mouse, but
say yes, und tole him pooty quiok.

MAMIE. [SIGHS.] Oh! dear. What shall I think?

DOCTOR. You vill do dot mooch, den you vill pesh mine fine
toughter, to make it goot in mine life und old age. You vill see on
der tay dot you pe coupled togetter py law, I vill get from der Count
fifty tousand tollars, den der Count und me und you vill go off Paris
all ofer to der bick Centennial. Den ve vill go in mine country und
look on der King's cashteel, und ve vill see all off der bick gounselmens und officers. You vill do dot mooch, von't you, in honor off
your fotter und his bick Toctor profession, von't you?

MAMIE. I am astonished, pa, that you should plan this match.

DOCTOR. Don'd you let dot motter off yours upset eferyting mit
her preaching to you apoud her notions off lofe, und her cold vater
und temperance, und her Shermans vat she don'd like. Don'd you
pay any attention to her Afrairican shtyle.

LUCY. [ASIDE] Give him an affirmative answer to every request
he makes.

DOCTOR. I go now to look after mine profession, und you coon
talk vat you blease.   [Departs.

MAMIE. What shall I do, mama? He is determined to dispose of
me in the same manner that your Aunt Lillabridge disposed of you.
Count Martrit is doubtless an unprincipled man; otherwise he would
never resort to such despicable trickery as papa just disclosed to obtain my hand; and then, too, he has never met me. Besides, if he
were what he pretends to be, he would hardly be found in such a dis-
reputable saloon as Fritz Grootenheimer's.

LUCY. Don't be alarmed, my dear Mamie. You shall never be his victim. I will always watch over and advise you.

MAMIE. Advise me quickly.

LUCY. Treat your father and the Count respectfully, and avoid giving them any offence. When the question of marriage arises, I shall act as the occasion seems to demand.

MAMIE. Well, it will be useless to try reasoning with papa. He is so headstrong.

LUCY. We shall have very little to say to him upon the subject.

MAMIE. I dread the interview with Count Martrit, and wish it were over.

LUCY. I feel positive that it will end unpleasantly, but the future can hardly bring forth darker shadows than the past. You shall never be compelled to marry a man who is intemperate, or otherwise unfitted to be your companion. It is enough that my life has been blighted; therefore I shall do all in my power to shield you from a like misfortune.

MAMIE. What shall we do if papa turns us out of doors?

LUCY. This property is mine, and if he ventures upon such a step, we shall return. I am willing to place my trust in Providence, firmly believing that whatever may happen will surely be for the better.

SCENE II.—LUCY'S Parlor. MAMIE is playing on the piano. LUCY and FAIRY are sitting listening to the music.

Enter the DOCTOR and COUNT MARTRIT.

The COUNT remains standing in the doorway. The DOCTOR quickly seizes FAIRY by the arm near the shoulder, raises her feet nearly from the floor and brings her before the COUNT, introducing her in the following manner, which makes FAIRY act frightened:

DOCTOR. Dis, Mishter—Sir—Herr—Count Martrit. Here, dis is mine leedle toughter, Fairy Pfeifer.

FAIRY. [BOWING.] Very happy to meet you, Sir Count Martrit.

COUNT. [BOWING.] Happy to meet you, Miss Fairy Pfeifer.

DOCTOR. [SHAKING FAIRY'S ARM.] You young shnips you. I help you mit "I'm happy to meet you." I tought I often tole you to shake hants. Done you know nottling? Dot is Afrairican shtyle, I should think. [LUCY AND MAMIE ACT AMAZED.—TO FAIRY.] Vat for you go off der school off you done even learn so moooh as to shake hants mit a shentlemans?   [FAIRY holds handkerchief to her eyes as if weeping. DOCTOR places FAIRY'S hand in the COUNT'S and says: "Shake hants und den po off und sit down." COUNT shakes hands with FAIRY. FAIRY sits down near LUCY.

DOCTOR. [SHOUTS TO LUCY.] Lucy, com't here. Halloo. [LUCY

GOES FORWARD.—INTRODUCES HER.] Mishter Count, dis is mine vife. [To LUCY.] Dis posh der Count Martrit, Mrs. Lucy Pfeifer. Make yourself acquainted. He is oud off Hanover, mine country. He is der Count from dare.

LUCY. [BOWING.] I am glad to form your acquaintance, Sir Martrit. Please be seated.   [COUNT sits down.

DOCTOR. [POLITELY.] Shake hants. Done you know notting? Dot is der vay laties in Shermany do.· [LUCY, with a perplexed look, shakes hands with the COUNT, excusing herself.

COUNT. Certainly.

DOCTOR. [To LUCY.] You tum peedle heat. Vat you mean py talking to de Count dot vay? Oh, shame on yourself. It's no vonder dot der shildrens act like fools. Make mit yourself oud, or go sit town.   [DOCTOR talks to MAMIE in a low tone.

LUCY. [To COUNT.] Please excuse the Doctor's remarks. You understood me, did you not?

COUNT. Most certainly I did. For my part, I beg you to feel entirely uncmbarrassed. [LUCY sits down by FAIRY. DOCTOR leaves MAMIE and goes towards the COUNT, calling and beckoning to the former.

DOCTOR. Mamie, coom. Mamie, coom't on here. Halloo. Shake hants mit der shentlemans. [MAMIE ADVANCES.] Now, Sir Count Martrit, dis is mine toughter, Miss Mamie Aldolfshtuff Alemedia Allesedia Pfeifer, but ve call her py her first name, Mamie. Make yourselfs acquainted mit him. Shake hants.

MAMIE. [SHAKES HANDS.] I'm glad to meet you, Sir Count.

DOCTOR. [PLEASED.] You pesh mine fine toughter, ha? You hafe more manners as der whole set putted togetter. [To COUNT.] You see, Mishter Sir Count, she pe pooty tall—dot means she shtants up pooty high—und ve hat to gife her pooty heafy names, und shtill she gets longer und longer. Pooty soon she shtops, ha?

COUNT. I have seen young ladies taller than Miss Pfeifer.
                    [All take seats.

MAMIE. How long will you remain in town?

COUNT. I intend to leave this evening at 10:15.

LUCY. How do you like America?

COUNT. Very much indeed.

DOCTOR. [To COUNT.] Mine toughter she is a fery coot fine blayer on der piano, und sings—she sings shoost like a pluejay.

COUNT. So I understood you to say yesterday.

DOCTOR. You know dose pluejays in Shermany?

COUNT. Yes.

DOCTOR. Dose pluejays vat fly rount in der vinter times, ofer der farms, picking up der corn-fielts vat trop rount here und dare? I dells you, she is shoost like vone off dose pluejays mit her fedders all pulled oud. Shoost so rich she looks.

COUNT. [To MAMIE.] Will you favor me with some musio, please?

MAMIE. Shall it be instrumental?

COUNT. I would prefer a song, knowing that you sing.

DOCTOR. Blay der piece vat I like apoud der moon.

MAMIE. It is so simplo that perhaps the Count wouldn't be pleased with it.

DOCTOR. [TO COUNT.] Oh, yes, yes, you'll like it pecause I do, von't you?

COUNT. Very well, I'll listen to your favorite.

[MAMIE plays " Come when the moonbeams softly glimmer." MAMIE. [TO COUNT.] Will you please join us in singing?

COUNT. What is the name of the song?

DOCTOR. It is, "Ven der moonpeams softly slimber." Dot means ven der moons goes off shleep.

MAMIE. The song is, " Come when the moonbeams softly glimmer."

DOCTOR. Titn't I tolo him like dot?

     [DOCTOR puts on spectacles, and then joins the COUNT in singing one verse. He holds the music so close to his own eyes that it is impossible for the COUNT to read the words, and acts ridiculously. When the chorus begins the COUNT sits down. The DOCTOR sings out of time and too high. When finishing the chorus, the DOCTOR asks the COUNT: " Done you tink I sing pooty goot for an olt man, und a man off mine profession?"

COUNT. You did sing very well indeed.

DOCTOR. I tink dot I sing shplendit. I hafe not hat sooch a voice for a long dime, in a goot many years. I tink dot dis coot singing vas all on der gount off your velcome. (TO MAMIE.] Coom, blay dot ofer vonce more, pecause I sing so goot.

MAMIE. I think once is sufficient, papa. I would rather be excused. [DOCTOR sits down, and then directs MAMIE to a chair very close to the COUNT.

DOCTOR. [TO MAMIE.] Sit yourself py der Count, so dot he can get vone goot look on you. I prought him here on dot purpose. In Shermany, ven shentlemans visit young laties, dey alvays sit vere ·dey can be seen. I tought you knew dot. I don't like to see young laties afraid off shentlemans.

MAMIE. [EMBARRASSED.] I feel quite comfortable where I am, papa.

COUNT. [TO MAMIE.] I notice that your papa tries to provide all that you require for your ease and comfort.

MAMIE. Yes, sometimes too much so to be agreeable.

DOCTOR. [TO COUNT.] Vat you tink off mine piano?

COUNT. It is a very loud sounding one.

DOCTOR. Yes, und ven Mamie blays mit der scales off der piano, dey go so quick as r-r-r-dt. You know how dot goes?

COUNT. I understand how they run the scales on a piano. [TO MAMIE.] You know the object of my visit, do you not?

MAMIE. Most certainly I do.

COUNT. [To DOCTOR.] As my time is limited, I must make my proposition now. May I have the hand of your daughter in marriage?

[All except the DOCTOR look surprised.

DOCTOR. Yes, yes, mit all off mine heart.

FAIRY. [To LUCY.] What does he mean, mama?

LUCY. Wait, and you will hear.

DOCTOR. [To COUNT.] Ofer dare is Lucy, mine vife. Ask her und den you pe all-right. She looks bleased to-tay.

COUNT. [To LUCY.] Dear madam, Doctor Pfeifer has consulted you regarding the union of your daughter and myself, which I suppose favorable. Do you object, or am I unworthy of your daughter?

LUCY. Sir Count, you will please overlook what may seem to you an inappropriate reply. Do not for one moment allow yourself to suppose we are not aware of the high honor which you would bestow upon my daughter, by taking her as your wife. I cannot see why you, who have always associated with the nobility should select an untitled wife, whose wealth is not equal to your own.

COUNT. I never considered your social standing. Will you consent to my proposition?

LUCY. Have you proposed to Mamie?

COUNT. No, madam. It is only necessary, in Germany, to obtain the consent of the parents.

LUCY. Well, it is different in this country. Here the daughter's preference is considered by her mother. We do not regard the young man's worldly possessions as of so much importance as his moral principles. We ask, " Is he temperate, and a true Christian?"

COUNT. Then you object, do you?

LUCY. I shall never consent to let Mamie become your wife. She is too young to think of taking such a responsibility upon herself. Under the circumstances, I feel impelled to disclose to you a vow which I made when Mamie was an infant.

COUNT. What was it, pray?

LUCY. It was this: Should she live to be a young lady, her happiness should never be blighted by act or word of mine.

COUNT. My dear madam, I have the consent of Doctor Pfeifer, and now it is only necessary to gain that of yourself and Mamie's to complete my happiness.

LUCY. Surely you, having only met her to-day for the first time, can have no deep affection for her.

COUNT. Dear madam, permit me to inform you that my father had never met my 'mother before the day they were married. Yet they always loved each other and lived happily.

LUCY. That may be true in their case, but it does not follow that it would prove to be the rule. I must say that my own life was blighted by being compelled to marry a stranger. From that day until the present time I have never known happiness, and I know that you could never be happy with my daughter without love.

[During LUCY's conversation with the COUNT, the DOCTOR
watches them both with an inquisitive air, and when
LUCY concludes he says to her: " It is petter off
you keep shtill."

DOCTOR. [To LUCY.] Oh! goot for notting. Vat is lofe? Coon
you tole me vat dot shtuff is? I pet you done know. I tole you so
often dot a man vat has a blenty off money coon lofe anypoty, und he
coon get a blenty off girls. It makes no tifference off he has gray
hair or not. I tole you so often, Lucy Pfeifer, dot vou shoult not
preach apout lofe to a man vat has a profession. Vat you tink dot
dey undershtand py lofe? It is money vat dey undershtand, und
shoost vat dey pe after. I know you coon't shplain vat lofe is, for I
hafe a profession und I coon't.

LUCY. Did you ever know that money without lofe never lasts
long?

DOCTOR. Vat you tink I care apout lofe? I got a pick profession.

COUNT. [To LUCY.] I had no intention of creating any trouble in
your family.

LUCY. You have a great advantage over Doctor Pfeifer in your
knowledge of English. We should exercise caution in conversing in
his presence, lest he may misunderstaud us.

COUNT. I shall occasion no further misunderstanding. I have
come simply as a gentleman to request your consent to my marriage
with your daughter.

LUCY. I decline to countenance your suit. Still there is Mamie.
You are at liberty to speak to her upon the subject. Let her answer
for herself.   [DOCTOR walks the room excitedly, when seeing the
          COUNT approach MAMIE, stops to listen to their
          conversation.

COUNT. [To MAMIE.] My dear Miss Pfeifer, you are doubtless
aware of the purpose of my visit. I have the consent of your father,
and your mother chooses to leave the decision with yourself. Shall
I have the happiness of having you return to my home with me?

MAMIE. No, sir. I have determined to pursue a course of stud-
ies already commenced, after which I shall feel better prepared for a
higher position in life.

COUNT. Will you not give me some hope?

MAMIE. To be candid about it, I never could love you.

COUNT. I can't see why you reject me. I would take you to Paris,
and from thence to Italy. I have already spoken to your father about
our traveling.

MAMIE. I understood papa to say that he met you in a saloon.

COUNT. [EXCITED.] Yes, yes—we met at his place of business.

MAMIE. I would not marry a man who frequents such places.

COUNT. I said that it was at your father's place of business.

MAMIE. Fritz Grootenheimer's saloon is not his place of business.

COUNT. I don't recollect where it was.

MAMIE. Some young men have very convenient memories.

COUNT. Now I remember, it was near a doorway that I met the Doctor.

DOCTOR. Vat funny folks I got, mit deir lofe. [TO MAMIE.] Who put dot foolishness apout lofe in your heat? Your motter? You tink I pring a becker here, dot ain't got notting, nor ain't got a profession like me?

MAMIE. Give me Paris with all of her riches and splendor, and I could never love him.

DOCTOR. She's shoost like her motter—all der dime tinking on her lofe—und neeter vone know vat lofe is. I'm sure I don'd. Pooh! pooh! Vat is dot, I like to know? It's shoost notting at all.

LUCY. I have known that for a long time. You love no one, nor will you allow any one to love you.

DOCTOR. Say, Lucy, do you lofe me? Shoost answer mine question pefore dis house.

LUCY. Do you want a candid reply?

DOCTOR. Yes, und right avay quick, so dat I coon undershtand you.

LUCY. Did I not inform you when my aunt compelled me to marry you?

DOCTOR. No, you ditn't. You run like crasy.

LUCY. I said then that I did not love you. You were nothing to me then, and because of your cruel treatment, you are nothing to me now. I told you that I had given my heart to my soldier boy, Deloss, before I met you, and that you could only have my hand. It was Deloss, a soldier boy, whom I loved, and I love him still. In my dreams I hold sweet communion with him, and in fancy rest my weary head upon his breast. It is that which gives me strength and courage to do my duties day by day until I can go hence to rejoin him beyond the clouds.

DOCTOR. Vat—you—you—lofe somepody else, und rest your heat on Deloss? I tought he is tead long ago. You rest your heat on an-otter man inshtead off on me? How coon you do dot, ven I tought he vas cone deat? [WITH RAGE, THROWS LUCY OUT OF THE DOOR.] Go now, und rest your heat on him out dare.

LUCY. [AS IF IN PAIN.] Oh, my head. [MAMIE and FAIRY act frightened. The COUNT gets his hat and stands still.

DOCTOR. [LEADS MAMIE TO THE DOOR.] I shlam you out toors, too, und nefer coom in here again, eeter. I'll see off you coon lofe oud dare. [FAIRY weeps and starts to run. DOCTOR leads her out,
saying: " Co vere you blease," and then closes door.

COUNT. Why did you turn your family out of doors?

[DOCTOR walks up and down the room, thumping his head as
if in trouble.

DOCTOR. Oh! vat an unlooky man I pesh.

Enter JOHNNY, who stares at the COUNT.

DOCTOR. [TO JOHNNY.] I clean house to-tay. Coom on. You go too.

JOHNNY. [WEEPS.] Where is my mama?

DOCTOR. [TO JOHNNY.] Coom, co fint tem off you coon. [PUTS HIM OUT.] Don't you tink I know how to clean house pooty goot for a man off mine profession? Don't you tink I'm a free man now? If you efer get married, don'd you nefer take an Afrairican voomans. [DRAWS REVOLVER.] I guess I get oud mine involver, [GOES TO DOOR] und see off I done a goot yob or not, und off I kilt der nations all or not. I see off I finished dem up. [SHOWS REVOLVER.] You see, Count, dot involver? She has apout five huntert shots in her. You pet I shoot 'em all dis time. [GOES OUT OF DOOR, AND THEN RETURNS.] Coom, coom. I coon't find dem anyvare oud dare. I guess dot dey vill sing apoud deir cold vaters und deir lofe somevare else inshtead off in dis house. Coom, coom. I co mit you on der drain for California.   [Departs with COUNT.

ACT XII.

SCENE I.

CHARACTERS—1. LUCY and her children.   2. LAWYER HOGAL.
3. 2d Lawyer.

LUCY is discovered lying on a couch, having FAIRY by the hand. JOHNNY sits at end of couch. MAMIE fans her mother. Door-bell rings.

MAMIE. [GOES TO DOOR.] Oh! that must be the lawyer.

Enter LAWYER with MAMIE.

LAWYER. Good morning, Mrs. Pfeifer. I am informed that you wish to see me on business. I am in a hurry, as court sits to-morrow and I have a present engagement elsewhere.

LUCY. Yes, I have very important business, having determined to apply for a divorce from Mr. Pfeifer. I have endured his cruelty for these many years, believing that God, in His own good time, would set me free. My suffering has been terrible, and I can bear it no longer.

LAWYER. I have the whole story. Please don't worry, dear madam. Your divorce will be granted by the next court.

[Children rejoice.

MAMIE. Oh! how glad I am.

LAWYER. [TO LUCY.] I wish you a speedy recovery. Good day, Mrs. Pfeifer. Call at my office next Wednesday.   [Departs.

SCENE II.—LAWYER HOGAL'S office.   MR. HOGAL at desk, writing.

Enter LUCY with daughters.

LAWYER. [OFFERS SEATS.] How do you do, Mrs. Pfeifer? We all had concluded that you were dead.

LUCY. Oh! no. I could not die. I have called to learn if I am freed from that madman or not.

Enter 2d Lawyer, who hands HOGAL papers and then departs.

LAWYER. [READS.] Lucy Pfeifer. Divorce granted from J. W. Pfeifer.

LUCY. Thank God. Free at last. Now I am no longer The Sold Orphan.

MAMIE. How does it seem to you now, mama?

LUCY. [TO ALL.] I feel like a caged eagle suddenly set free. Had I the eagle's wings, I would soar aloft, and in shouting my freedom to the world, dare the tyrant to touch or harm me now.

www.ingramcontent.com/pod-product-compliance
Lightning Source LLC
Chambersburg PA
CBHW030853260626
47169CB00008B/2518